CHINWE

Books by Peter Burchard

CHINWE
by Peter Burchard

with drawings by the author

G. P. Putnam's Sons · New York

For Lee and Laura
with much love

Library of Congress Cataloging in Publication Data
Burchard, Peter. Chinwe.
SUMMARY: Captured by slave traders, a young Ibo girl,
her brother and their fellow villagers suffer hardships
and cruel treatment on their way to the New World where
they are sold as slaves.
1. Slave trade—Fiction. 2. Ibo tribe—Fiction.
I. Title.
PZ7.B9159Cf [Fic] 78-24401
ISBN 0-399-20667-1

Acknowledgments

Thanks to the staffs of the G. W. Blunt White Library and the Curatorial Department at Mystic Seaport for assistance in gathering material for this book. A special vote of thanks to Emily Wharton for giving freely of her time and counsel and to Chinwe Ezenekwe for willingly giving much needed advice. Last, but by no means least, thanks to Marion Putzel for valuable editorial help.

Part I
THE VILLAGE

I

It was shortly after midnight. Chinwe awakened with a start, her heart beating wildly. At first she kept her eyes closed, listening, touching the dry, red earth. Then, to reassure herself, she opened her eyes, but the shapes of familiar things in the hut and the light of the stars gave way to ugly, twisted visions. She had dreamed of hordes of warriors, led by men with pale, white skins, attacking her village and crashing through the gate.

Chinwe rose up and stepped outside her family's hut. She was tall and muscular, her breasts firm, her skin a dark luminescent brown. The other huts, all round and squat, were dark against the deep night sky. She looked toward the walls of the village which encircled the dwellings. The surrounding fields and orchards were quiet. A squawk of death came out of the forest, the voice of a bush hen surprised by a cat.

She wondered if Azu was still on guard outside the walls. Azu was the eldest son of the headman, Okudu, and commanded the men who stood around the village, protecting it from the raids of slave hunters and other hostile, warring tribes.

Chinwe called her dog, softly, so as not to waken the rest of the family. She called again and at last he came loping toward her and jumped up against her leg. She went back inside and lay down as the animal settled nearby on her mat. She pulled him close, feeling the wetness of his nose.

She looked through the doorway at the stars, noticing patterns she had seen before. She thought again of Azu, of his long, lean body and his quick smile. Then, remembering her dream, she felt a flash of fear for his safety. Was he sleeping now or guarding the gate? She hoped he was sleeping in the darkness of his hut.

Her fear was deepened by the knowledge that tomorrow her father would go on another of his journeys. Though her father was young, because he traveled, his opinion was valued, not only by the elders and by Okudu, but by Chukwuemeka, the chief of the tribe and known to many Ibo people. Once, he had gone as far as the ocean. He had been in constant danger of capture by the Salt Water People, who traded in slaves as others traded in palm oil and gold.

Chinwe knew her father's travels were important, but the sharpness of her dream, her deep forebodings, made her wish he would not go now.

2

The village was stirring.

Chinwe sat up. Her dog was gone, probably following the smell of cooking. Chinwe bathed her eyes and wrapped a cloth around her hips. She reached for a charm her father had given her, a sea shell, white with a polished orange mouth, suspended from a goatskin thong. She looped the thong around her neck, stepped outside and greeted her parents.

Breakfast in front of her family's hut was one of the pleasures of the day. Chinwe's little sister Jagua, lively and happy, was seldom still. Chinwe watched as she scampered away. Her brother Odili, who was quieter than most of the boys his age, listened as Chinwe, Mother and Father talked. His dark eyes moved as he watched their faces. Sometimes he smiled, often not at what he heard but as if at a secret of his own. He was liked and respected by the other boys. He was fleet of foot and he was brave.

On the days of his departures, Father was quiet,

expressing his love in the smallest of ways. He sat straight up, glancing at Mother as she moved about the fire.

Mother was a beauty, more so because she was great with child. Her neck was long. Her face proud. Chinwe wished she could talk to her mother as she would to a sister, but many years of pain and pleasure ran like the waters of a river between them. Even now, as Mother sat across from Father, filling the bowls with cereal and honey, Chinwe could see the pain in her face, brought by thoughts of Father's departure. Mother turned to him, avoiding his eyes but speaking as one who had a right to speak. "Come back, if you can, before the rains."

"I will try. First, I must visit Chukwuemeka. Then I will visit an Aro priest."

Chinwe knew that the Aro were an arrogant, often dangerous, people, that many were corrupt, that some of them sold their own people into slavery. "May the god of our fathers keep you safe," she said, touching one of her bright gold earrings. "Will you leave as I go with the women to the fields?"

"Later," he said. "When the sun is high."

"Do you think the danger to our tribe increases?"

Father shrugged. "We shall see," he said. "White men in distant lands want slaves. They buy them from the Salt Water People. The tricks of the Salt Water People are many."

"What can we do against men like that, men who are armed with muskets and pistols?"

"We will organize patrols. Our drums will talk in secret tongues. Our warriors will gather to attack slave columns."

"Why have we not done this before?"

Father only shook his head.

Mother said proudly, but in a voice that lacked conviction, "Our village is safe. The ditch around the walls is wide and deep. The best young men are guarding the gate."

Father glanced across at the place where old men played their games of trade. "We must do more than wait," he said.

Chinwe and her father stood together. His gaze met hers. "Goodbye, Chinwe."

"Goodbye, my father."

3

After a day of work in the fields, Chinwe walked toward the village with Idoto, who chattered too much about the weaving she was doing, and Ifeoma, who was Chinwe's best friend. Idoto's face was wide and her teeth slanted outward. Ifeoma, on the other hand, was pretty. Her hair was short and parted in the middle. She wore a small fetish, like a butterfly, at her hairline, just in the center of the part. Chinwe always listened when Ifeoma spoke because Ifeoma was thoughtful and quietly funny.

Chinwe tolerated Idoto but Idoto was tiresome. And Idoto was jealous and sometimes bitter.

The women crossed a piece of fallow ground, walked between two fields of grain, all gold and still in the afternoon sun, and approached the gate where Azu and his brother Obi stood. Azu smiled. He held his spear above his head and Chinwe copied him, raising her arm as he had raised his.

Idoto, who nursed a love for Azu, turned away and looked toward the forest.

Obi was nearly as tall as Azu. His nose was broader at its base. Both were lean and muscular but the two were very different. Obi had a dark and somber nature. Obi's eyes, like Azu's, were bright but he had a hard and brooding mouth.

Azu stood apart, not only from his brother but from the other men as well. It wasn't just his height that set him apart. When Chinwe was close by, most young men grew shy or sullen. One of them, a painfully skinny, silent youth, narrowed his eyes, watching Chinwe as he might have watched a lizard. Another giggled foolishly and chattered. Azu, on the other hand, regarded her with frank admiration and, no matter how much he might smile and talk, when he bid her goodbye, he was solemnly respectful. Knowing the answer before he asked the question, Azu asked, "Will you dance tonight, Chinwe?"

Chinwe, replying, moved her feet then, aware that Idoto was openly jealous, straightened up and nodded. "So will Idoto and Ifeoma," she said.

The women passed through the gate and went their separate ways. Chinwe walked toward her family's hut, watching the caterwauling children by the market, all screaming like hawks drifting toward a carcass. Chinwe's brother Odili raced against two other boys.

Like the others, her family's hut was a circular construction of stakes and mud, decorated with vertical stripes and topped by a cone-shaped roof of leaves and grass. Carved wooden houseposts guarded its door. As Chinwe approached the hut, she saw her sister, with her hair all done in intricate designs, playing with another child in the dust. She looked up, making a comic face, eyes a deep and liquid brown, before she returned to what she was doing, making a pattern of sticks and leaves, around two round black stones.

Chinwe ducked through the doorway. Outside, Mother was cutting up a melon. "Did Father leave as expected?" Chinwe asked.

"He did," Mother said, putting down her knife and standing as straight as her condition would let her. Chinwe expected her mother to be sad, but her face was happy. Her mother turned away and went to one of the hampers by the wall of the hut. Chinwe and the little ones never touched the hampers. Father's held ceremonial things, body paint, clothing and heavy masks, kept for extraordinary occasions. Chinwe had warned them about the masks. If a woman looked into the face of a mask, she risked sickness or death. Father smiled when he mentioned such things, but he obeyed the customs of his people.

Uncovering her hamper, Mother took out an assortment of garments and brightly colored ornaments. Her eyes shining, Mother gave Chinwe the things she had made, garters, bangles and a waistband to wear when she danced.

Chinwe could scarcely believe her eyes. She had lacked the cloth and dyes, feathers and beads, to make these things, and the ones she had were stained and faded. She held the treasures in the sunlight in the doorway, turning them over, admiring their beauty. She laid them across a stool and from the top of the pile took a ring of rattles and feathers, slipped the garter around an ankle and, looking down at the brilliant colors, moved her feet, making barely audible music. She imitated a dance of the men, part of the climax of a dance of war.

Watching her daughter imitate the men, aware of her wickedness, Mother's eyes grew wide. Chinwe finished the dance and began to laugh. Then her mother softened and she too laughed, gently pressing the sides of her stomach.

Chinwe took off the rattle, put it with the other things and faced her mother, and looked into her eyes. "Thank you, my mother."

Chinwe rubbed her body with palm oil, put on her golden raffia skirt and her new decorations. Showing off her costume, Chinwe stood tall while Mother and Sister made sounds of approval. Chinwe's brother Odili was lost in admiration, fingering and pulling at a bright yellow feather.

Chinwe said, "Mind you don't pull it off, Odili."

Mother, proud of her work and a little short of temper, said, "Stop that, Odili! Leave Chinwe's skirt as it is."

Odili subsided and sat in a corner. This suddenly seemed a solemn occasion. Mother was wistful. She had danced, not long ago. Now, as if she were sick, she must stay in the hut, listening, wishing she could dance with the others. Then, apparently thinking of the coming of the baby, she smiled at Chinwe. "Never mind," she said. "My time will soon come. I'll soon be leaving the baby with you."

Knowing mother was joking, Chinwe flashed a happy smile. She glanced at Odili, teasing him. "Odili can mind the baby," she said.

Odili stood up and bared his teeth. "I want to dance with the men," he said.

Chinwe laughed. "In any case, tonight you will go."

Sister said, "I want to go tonight."

Chinwe said gently, "You must wait. Your turn will come next year."

4

Chinwe and Odili passed the boabob tree inside the gate, where the headman stood with Azu, Obi and his younger sons. They worked back along the column, first passing the elders, then the warriors, married women and older men. Chinwe left Odili with a young married neighbor and took her place with the maidens, whose costumes were very much like hers, though not as beautiful or bright. She soon became the object of sidelong glances, longing glances of the men who passed by, looks of envy from the women. Chinwe responded with quiet self-assurance.

As the sun dipped red behind the trees, the column moved out through the gate and spilled across the dancing ground. The people formed a ring around the drummers, six muscular men, three of them holding long tubular drums, three sitting in front of larger drums, made of tree trunks and supported by stubby wooden legs.

Surrounded by his sons and by the elders, Okudu sat serenely on a rickety chair fashioned out of bamboo, thongs and cloth. Using a spear decorated with varicolored streamers, Okudu stood up and gave a lofty signal. All at once the villagers were silent. As Azu raised his musket, pointed at the sky and fired, Chinwe felt a thrill of pride. Azu had taught her how to load and fire his musket, one of only three muskets in the village.

As a trail of smoke rose up from the gun, the tallest of the standing drummers tapped out a series of single beats, followed by a pause. The second standing drummer beat an answering signal and, joined by the others, brought forth a labyrinth of sound, as ten young men, naked but for loincloths and garters, holding rattles, moved away from the ring of people, forming a circle around the drummers.

The larger drums thundered and the men began to dance.

The proudest of the men were Azu and Obi. The two led the others as they circled the drummers, dancing a complicated step and beginning another, quicker dance.

Watching Azu, admiring his body, the flatness of his chest and belly, Chinwe felt a sweet, sharp rush of desire. She, Idoto, Ifeoma and the other maidens chanted, keeping time with the drums and the rattles. A rhythmic cry, a great chorus of voices rose above the ground where the young men danced and the feet of the dancers moved ever more swiftly as the cadence of the drumbeats gained momentum. The dancers chanted, answering the watchers, lifting their faces to the darkening sky. When the dancers finished their sixth encirclement, the drums rose to a sudden crescendo and stopped.

As the young men quit, a boy carrying a flaming torch skirted the drummers, lighting piles of wood and straw surrounding the dancing ground, lighting smaller fires around the drummers. The drums sounded once again and the young men danced a second time, followed by the maidens and the children. Chinwe's feet flashed in the flickering light. She became a part of a swift bright river made up of the feathers and the streamers of the people.

Okudu called out once again and the people fell silent. The drummers repeated Okudu's call and the people fell back again, clearing the ground for pairs of richly costumed dancers, men and women as mates, who moved with extraordinary grace. Two came as bush fowl, a hen and a cock, two as creatures of the jungle, a panther and his mate, and two as goats, the man wearing a pair of wooden horns.

As the dancers approached it, the ground was clear, reflecting the firelight.

Again, the tallest of the drummers tapped, the thunder of the tall drums rumbled and the dancers danced a mating dance, familiar to all but the youngest of the children.

Chinwe watched the children's faces, concentrating at last on Odili, whose eyes, as he tried to understand the dance, were as big as the eyes of a bullock.

The men encircled their mates, each sounding a wooden whistle. The dance became a dance of copulation. Had it not been so formal, so skillfully done, it might have made Chinwe want to laugh, but instead she found it touching and, as the dancers drifted apart, lapsing into a listless trance, she brushed away a tear.

At last, they circled once again, each one dancing a lonely step, with a faintly melancholy expression.

Chinwe's heart pounded as she, Ifeoma, Idoto and seven other maidens advanced toward the drummers, as if spreading seeds, sowing imaginary fields. Though she knew that Azu was watching her closely, Chinwe's feet moved with incredible ease. Aware of her attractiveness, she nonetheless displayed it with grace, much as Azu had displayed his manhood.

The firelight reddened and began to wane as the maidens danced another step, suggesting the cutting and threshing of grain.

Now the ten young men who had started the dancing joined the maidens as if exulting in a

bountiful harvest, dancing wildly, shriek
against a thundering crescendo.

As the final dance ended, the boy with the torch
lit a fire in front of Okudu and Okudu raised his
spear again. At first, in the hush that followed his
gesture, Chinwe heard only the whisper of the
fires. Okudu seemed reluctant to speak. He
seemed only to listen. Now Chinwe heard it. A
drum in a neighboring village was talking.

A VILLAGE DOWNRIVER WAS BURNED TODAY

When Okudu spoke, his voice was like the
sound of a distant drum. "We trust our own
priests. Long ago, they traveled to the land of
Aro, the place where Chukwa, the oracle, lives.
Chukwa gave them the word of our god. Ever
since, they have preached his word." Okudu
trembled with emotion. "But many of the priests
in the land of Aro were long ago corrupted by a
lust for riches, the white man's rum and the white
man's weapons. These priests, pretending to
preach the word of God, lie to their people, telling
them God demands the blood of his children,
pretending to sacrifice people to Chukwa, selling
them instead to the Salt Water People who sell
them in turn to the captains of the slavers."

At first the villagers were silent. Some of the
older people nodded. Many knew about these
things and began to talk among themselves.

23

Again, the headman signaled for silence. "Now the time we have feared is here. The Salt Water People, once poor, are now rich, but it seems that their greed has increased with their riches. Many have war canoes and guns. Many are tired of dickering with priests."

Okudu glanced at a cluster of children. He cocked his head, looking toward his two tall sons. "Load your muskets. I will load mine. Every able-bodied man must grind his spear, his arrowheads. Double the guard outside our gates. Eight of the fastest and bravest of our boys will go to the forest and hide beside the paths, and run to the gate if an enemy approaches. My older sons will examine the weapons and lead the men. My youngest son will be one of the watchers."

In response to Okudu's willingness to risk the life of his youngest son, a murmur arose from the people of the village.

Okudu nodded and raised both arms. "May our god and the father of us all, our common ancestor, protect us. May the fruit of our ancestors cover the earth."

5

Chinwe stood with Idoto, under a stand of iroko trees, wielding wooden pestles like paddles, punching them into bowls of millet, flailing the dry stalks, beating out the grain. Chinwe's arms ached but she liked this better than kneeling in the fields. Mostly the women worked the earth, raising yams, cassava, okra and ground nuts, while the men worked the orchards.

At last came the voice of the drum by the gate, the signal to come in from the fields. Two young mothers, working close by, picked up their babies from mats on the ground and put them to their breasts. Chinwe touched her hips, feeling the dampness of her red waistcloth. She walked with the others across the fallow fields, along a path through a stand of uncut grass and across the ground where the people of the village had danced last night.

Azu was standing by the gate. Chinwe smiled as she approached, absentmindedly reaching for the charm at her breast. The seashell her father had given her was gone. Breathlessly, she said, "Idoto!"

"What is it, Chinwe?"

"I've lost the shell my father gave me."

"You must have dropped it. Look for it tomorrow."

"I value it highly."

Azu asked about the loss, and as Chinwe explained about the shell, he glanced at the men who stood beside him. "I will leave the gate long enough to look for the shell. Chinwe and I can retrace her steps."

Idoto said quickly, "And I will go with you."

Chinwe smiled at Idoto's response and the three set out to look for the shell, walking toward the trees where the women had worked, Azu holding his long, slim spear. Chinwe searched the ground while Idoto watched Azu, who scanned the fields and the bush beyond, looking for signs of danger in the forest. No neighboring drums had sounded that day, or if they had, the noises of the village and the chatter of animals and birds had drowned them out.

The three traversed the uncut field and slowly crossed the fallow ones. Chinwe scanned the path and grass beside it. "I hope I didn't drop it here," she said. "The grass at the side of the path is thick."

Idoto said, "Wasn't it a common kind of shell?"

26

Chinwe said, "No, I'd never seen one like it before."

Azu turned back, speaking softly. "It must be under the trees," he said.

They went toward the trees where the bowls and tools were stacked, Azu squinting, examining the forest. At the foot of the tree, he knelt for a moment and picked up something from the ground.

Chinwe took the shell, thanking Azu, and held it, admiring it a moment before she tied it around her neck. As he stood there, Azu stared at the sky above the highest leaves of the forest.

All three saw a pall of smoke, far away, drifting and thinning. Idoto asked, "What is it?"

Thinking of the message of the drums, remembering her dream, Chinwe drew a quick short breath. "I think it's one of the villages in flames." As she spoke, she heard a scream in the forest and one of the boys who was watching the paths ran in Azu's direction. "I heard the sound of feet," he said. The boy stared wildly back at the forest, then turned and ran across the fields toward the gate. Idoto, Chinwe and Azu turned to follow but stopped at the sound of a rasping voice.

Three men emerged from the darkness of the trees. All were black as a magpie's wing, all were armed with muskets or spears.

Azu had a whistle on a string around his neck

27

and, as he lifted it toward his lips, the tallest stranger raised his musket. Azu was unafraid. His voice was deep. "Will you kill us?" he asked.

The man seemed not to understand. The others were sullen.

Azu pointed to the smoke above the trees. The tallest man glanced at the smoke and nodded, grinning. He gestured toward the path that led to their village, seeming to say that their village was next.

Suddenly Azu was a man gone mad. As quick as a lightning flash, he threw his spear, hitting the tall man high in the belly. The man fell to the earth, his two companions raised their muskets and other men appeared at the edge of the forest. Now Azu and the maidens were surrounded. Azu reached for the knife in the sheath at his hip, but before he could touch it, one of the attackers fired his musket and Azu paused, as if surprised, looking down at a rush of blood at his hip.

Azu's wound appeared to be shallow, but he staggered and fell and, as he started to rise, another man jumped him brandishing a knife.

Chinwe flew at Azu's attacker but before she could reach him he drew the knife across Azu's throat. Azu's attacker straightened up, sucking in furious draughts of air, baring broken yellow teeth, while Chinwe rushed toward him lashing out with her fists. The man cupped his hand and struck Chinwe, sending her sprawling. Chinwe had never been hit by a man and she lay in pain on the hard dry earth before she gained her feet again and saw that Idoto stood transfixed, looking down at Azu, making guttural sounds in her throat.

Azu's eyes stared into the heavens and a river of blood ran away from his neck, forming a thick red pool on the ground. Chinwe gave a long, last, desperate cry and, crumpled at Azu's side, putting her cheek against his chest.

Chinwe felt someone pulling at her arm. Idoto squatted near Azu's feet, staring blankly at his legs, tugging at Chinwe, imploring her to stand aside. Caught in a rising torrent of rage, Chinwe turned on Idoto and said, "He is dead."

Slowly, Idoto sank to the ground, nodding and weeping, and Chinwe, with a mixture of anger and desperation, took Idoto's hand and helped her rise. One of the attackers approached the women, and using the handle of his spear as a prod, drove them toward the trunk of a tree. With the help of another, he tied them fast to one of its branches.

Chinwe, straining at her bonds, stared at the attackers emerging from the forest, all armed, all bent in attitudes of war, advancing toward the village.

Idoto looked toward the village where her

mother, father and brothers were, then gave Chinwe a half-crazed stare and said in a voice like the hiss of a snake, "Azu died to find your shell."

Chinwe said nothing. She tugged at her bonds until she knew she would cut herself if she continued.

Staring again at Azu's body, watching the slave hunters pass it by, Chinwe remembered the single day they had spent alone together. They had made up praise names for each other. He was as graceful as a leopard and, laughing as he'd said it, he had called her as light as a bird's breast feathers. As tears began to streak her cheeks, she thought of the bravery of the man she loved. Azu's name would be a legend in the village. Okudu would praise him when he spoke to his people. The men of the tribe would sing about him, first man to die in defense of his village.

These thoughts faded as she opened her eyes. For a moment she looked like a woman whipped as she faced the stark reality. Azu's name had died with his body, and Okudu himself, too old to be a slave, would soon be dead.

As the cries of battle reached her ears and smoke rose high above the village, Chinwe stood stiff against the tree. Her mother, her brother and sister might survive. She might see them again, but the village and many of its people, its animals, her dog, her mother's goat, the cows, bullocks and chickens, all would die before tomorrow. Her father might be dead already, but even if he lived, unless she could free herself, live in the forest and seek him out, she knew she was never to see him again. If Father was living, he would surely come back here. But if he came, he would find the charred remains of huts, a bowl or two, perhaps some tools and the tree by the market with a twist in its trunk. She shied away from thoughts of the dead. These men would never bury the dead.

Having faced the truth, Chinwe trembled. Above the roar of the fires and the battle, she heard the piercing scream of a woman. As the sound cut deep, echoing, fading, Chinwe said softly, "As the sun will rise again, so will I rise. So will I live."

6

Darkness crept across the sky as other captives were brought to the fields. Chinwe knew most of them by name, many were cousins, close neighbors or friends. Gentle Ifeoma, Chinwe's best friend, came like one of a herd of cattle, driven by a man with a face like a rock. Ifeoma looked neither to her right nor left. Her eyes were the eyes of a sightless woman, her mouth a loose and lifeless thing. Across the way, Azu's brother Obi crouched on a patch of bare red earth, joined to other men with collars and chains. Their necks were manacled but only the ankles of Obi were shackled. Obi must have given his captors trouble. He had a welt across his forehead, but though his neck and cheek were caked with blood, his chin was high and his face was hard.

There were prisoners who still had the strength to grieve for a child or a mate who had died in the fighting. Some wept without sobbing, others cried aloud and moaned. Some captives talked, but when they talked too much they were kicked and whipped.

Against the dying light of the sun, a boy walked close, Chinwe called out and Odili ran to her. He clung to her silently, breathing hard. Chinwe was anxious to know what he had seen, whether their mother and sister were living, but instead of asking she nuzzled his cheek.

A slave hunter saw that Odili was free and came to take him away from Chinwe.

Chinwe said, "Please. He is my brother."

Odili clutched her, tighter than before, and the man began to laugh, pointing at Odili and Chinwe, talking in a foreign dialect.

It was clear that the man thought Chinwe was Odili's mother. He shrugged, moved off and returned with lengths of chain and collars, chained them together and bound them in turn to other women and their children. The women's hands were left free.

The guards lit fires around the fields and kept them burning with stalks of millet and pieces of deadwood taken from the forest. As the firelight rose, Chinwe remembered last night's fires, the distant happy dances, the joys of a life that had suddenly, violently, ceased to exist.

Chinwe dozed and woke up while Odili slept. Watching the glow in the sky above the village, she remembered her nightmare of night before last. This was worse by far than her dream.

Odili woke up as the stars began to fade. He cried. Chinwe sat up, put his head in her lap and glanced again at Obi, whose battered face revealed his rage.

Chinwe toyed with her collar and, feeling the shell and its thong underneath it, untied the thong and tied it instead around her wrist. Odili lifted his collar, to see if he could take it off, and found it large enough so he could.

Chinwe said, "Leave it as it was."

"I want to go back to the village now."

Chinwe spoke sharply. "No," she said. "Promise you will stay with me."

He searched her face and nodded. "I will," he said softly. "I promise to stay with you, Chinwe."

The sun mounted the sky, and the slave hunters went among the people, giving each a dollop of meal and a mouthful of water. The slave hunters cooked and ate chickens and goat's meat stolen from the village and, after eating and drinking their fill, prodded the captives into columns.

Obi, close to where Chinwe was standing, near the tail of a coffle, turned toward the pall of smoke still above the village, then stared at one of the men he was chained to, a man whose head was bent in shame. Obi told him, "Straighten your back."

34

A slave hunter flicked his whip at Obi. The coffle began to move.

Despite the weight of his collar, Odili held himself straight and Chinwe said, "Good. We must be brave."

Suddenly Odili asked, "Where is Father? Is he dead?"

"I wish I could tell you."

Weakly, almost timidly, Chinwe asked Odili if Mother was dead.

Odili nodded.

"Is Sister dead too?"

Again he nodded.

Chinwe's hope had been small. Now her hope lay still.

For the first time since she'd vented her hatred, Idoto spoke to Chinwe. "Where are they taking us," she asked.

"I think to the sea."

"Do you think we might escape?"

"No. Not now."

Guards, exhausted after the fierceness of yesterday's battle, angry that their brothers had been killed in the fighting, moved along the columns, whipping and prodding. As they entered the forest, the captives sang a mournful dirge. Once again, Chinwe looked back and, this time, saw a flight of vultures, hovering, wheeling, above the village, dipping into its smoking ruins.

Part II
THE RIVER

I

As the column approached the Niger River, the coffle of women broke away from the men and moved along a jungle path, toward a bright-green stretch of riverbank.

Chinwe and the others stopped in their tracks as a baboon family, almost winging, skittered through the underbrush, their swift, soft fur like burnished gold. One of the little ones, his white tail curling, vaulted a cluster of dark, green leaves studded with orange and yellow flowers, lost his balance and came down hard, sprawling on a patch of earth.

Odili laughed as the dog-faced creature, dazed and unsteady, picked himself up, stared wildly once around and moved away in pursuit of his mother. His laughter lightened Odili's spirits, but as they came to the water he frowned. "Will they make us swim the river?"

"I think not, Odili. The river is full of crocodiles."

"Where are they taking us, Chinwe?"

"I told you, Odili. I think to the sea."

The women and children sat on the bright green riverbank. The men were just upstream from the women and one of them began to chant. When other men joined him, one of the slave hunters shouted for silence. Most of the voices faded and died, but the voice of the man who had started the singing rose to a high, melodic shout and, all at once, became a scream of pain.

"What has happened?" Odili asked.

Chinwe said shortly, "Why is it you talk so much, Odili?"

"What has happened?" Odili repeated.

Idoto said, "Hush, Odili. Hush." The man cried out again and was silent. Chinwe said, "One of the guards has taught us a lesson."

"Singing is not an offense against God."

Chinwe looked into her brother's eyes. "Odili?" she said.

"What is it, Chinwe?"

"I'm sorry I asked why you talk so much."

As the sun touched the tops of the trees across the river, Odili slept while Chinwe and Idoto sat quietly together. Chinwe regretted her annoyance with Idoto. Now Idoto's hopeless love for Azu was suddenly endearing. Chinwe reached out to touch her hand but Idoto drew her hand away and turned toward the river.

"Now we are sisters in grief," Chinwe said.

Idoto, still without smiling, nodded, gazing across the wide brown waters.

The women were tired, but many had babies and children to think of, many of whom were hungry and cried.

The captain of the slave hunters walked along the grassy bluff. His beard was black. His body was fat. His face was set in a perpetual frown.

The air was heavy with the smell of blossoms. Some of the slave hunters, talking together, walked among the trees and gathered fruit and nuts.

Six others went down to the water's edge and into a grove of closely spaced trees. Shouting to each other, pulling and pushing, they brought out a war canoe, high and pointed at its ends, decorated with bold designs, bright red, tender green and white.

Five men paddled the canoe, driving it across the water. As it moved upstream, caught in the mirrored light, going against the river's current, the canoe lost speed and the sixth man threw a net across the water. The net hovered, still for a moment, caught in the fiery glow of the sun, before it mushroomed, dropped and sank and the fisherman pulled and gathered it toward him. He did this twice and once again, the last time shouting to the others. This time the net, boiling, streaming in the wake of the vessel, was alive with fishes, silver and blue.

Chinwe despised these Salt Water People, but despite her hatred, watching their graceful, muscular backs, she admired their skillful ways as they beached the canoe and all six dragged the net toward the bluff. One large fish jumped clear of the trap, making Chinwe think again of escape.

Odili asked, "Will we march again tomorrow?"

"I think they will take us to the sea in canoes."

Idoto said, "I want to die. I've heard the white men will kill us and eat us."

Chinwe said, "Sometimes I think I want to die but not because I expect to be eaten. Don't tell the others the white men will eat them. If you do, they will try to kill themselves."

"It is true."

"It is not. We are worth more to them as slaves than as cattle."

2

In the twilight, the fishermen cleaned their fish
and cooked them over blazing fires. One of the
younger ones, wearing a bright gold snake
around his arm, walked among the women,
carrying sacks of coconuts and melons, giving out
food to the women and children. As he stopped in
front of Chinwe and Idoto, his manner was kind
and his voice was strong. Even though he spoke
in a tongue that was much like hers, Chinwe had
trouble understanding what he said. When he
spoke, she nodded, regarding him coolly. She
asked him for water, but instead of giving her
what she had asked for, he laid a coconut on the
grass and, using a bush knife, with a single deft
stroke split the coconut end to end, spilling some
of its milk on the ground.

Odili opened his eyes and watched as the man
laid the second coconut down, raised his knife
and brought it down. He gave them half a coconut
each, and when Odili thanked him, the man

reached into his sack again, gave them each a melon and a handful of nuts and moved away, looking back several times at Chinwe.

Idoto whispered, "Be careful, Chinwe. The man is kind because of you."

One of the fishermen distributed fish and, as the captives finished supper, the cooking fires became islands of light. The forest was black and the river was broad, streaked in the middle where the current ran strong.

In the flickering, waning light of the fires, Odili slipped his collar off, stood up and stretched as if preparing to move away. Chinwe took his wrist and pulled him down. "Odili, put your collar back on."

"Some of the children are free," he said.

"They are younger. Stay close."

Chinwe handed Odili his collar, thinking that if somehow she could free herself, she and Odili could steal away and live in the forest. If Father was alive, perhaps they could find him and live in another village like theirs. Her thoughts were interrupted by the voice of the man who had given them the coconuts and melons. "Quick, Odili!" Chinwe said. "Slide into your collar. If the slave hunters know it is loose, they will fix it."

Odili did as he was told. The man stopped close to a woman with a baby and laid an empty sack on the ground, making a place for the baby to lie. He moved in front of Chinwe and nodded, speaking slowly and distinctly. "This boy is your brother, is he not?"

Chinwe nodded, avoiding his eyes, watching his feet, wishing his feet would go away. One foot moved. The other was still. At last he sat down. "Soon the rains will come," he said.

"I have no stomach for talk of rains. You killed our mother and the child inside her. You killed our sister, four years old.".

"I have never killed," he said.

"I see. You play a vulture's game."

The man stood up. He spoke in a hard, metallic voice. "Why should I listen to you?" he said.

"Why do you kill and enslave our people?"

"I too am a slave."

"You wear no chains but you do the will of a master. Why?"

"We are the best of the slaves of our king. We who man our master's canoes are working for our freedom. Someday I may have slaves of my own."

"Have you no courage? What a sheep you are! Do you want to be a master? Why not simply be free?"

He answered only Chinwe's second question. "Yes," he said. "I want to be a master."

As the man moved off, Idoto spoke in an unsteady voice. "You should have kept quiet."

As the captives grew quiet, the guards began to speak in whispers. Chinwe stretched out on the grass. Idoto, lying an arm's length from Chinwe,

45

settled down to sleep. A baby in the coffle cried and then stopped. One woman wept, shedding mournful, bitter tears.

Chinwe thought of Azu and the man he had been. Even for a herd of goats, for glittering jewels and many wives, Azu, if he'd had a choice, would never have remained a slave. The kindness of the man who had given them food seemed no more than a handful of dust.

Odili moved closer and, feeling his warmth, Chinwe lay still and gazed at the stars. She picked out complicated designs, but try as she would, she failed to find the patterns she had seen in the village.

Idoto's breathing was shallow and steady. Odili sighed and fell asleep and, knowing he was sleeping, Chinwe was lonely. The sky became a blur. She slept.

She was awakened by the touch of a hand on her arm. She opened her eyes and saw the shape of the man who had fed them. As she turned away, he fumbled for her hand, and when she pulled it back, he touched one of her breasts.

"My body is mine," she said. "Leave my brother and me alone."

The man rose slowly and stood against the sky.

Odili woke up and asked in a faint and rasping voice, "Did you dream, Chinwe?"

Chinwe touched his head, felt for his shoulder and caressed it softly. "Go to sleep, my Odili," she said.

Idoto stirred but lay as before.

The man made an ugly sound and moved away.

Odili asked, "Who was that, Chinwe?"

"The man who fed us. Go to sleep, Odili."

"You sleep too. Remember the song Father sang about the river?"

"The river cuts a path through the forest."

"The river joins the great salt sea."

Odili settled down again while Chinwe lay awake and listened to the deep, barely audible roar of the river. The moon was bright above the bank, shimmering in the surface of the water.

Chinwe scanned the riverbank, feeling the man was watching, waiting. At last, hearing only the song of the frogs, her breathing slowed and she thought about her father. Somehow she knew her father was living. Chinwe clung to a belief in her god, whom she knew lived far above the dangers of the earth, but her belief in a life after death had been shaken. Could a death like Azu's, at the hands of people whose god was also Azu's god, be simply a passage? Despite her doubts, she spoke directly to her god. "Let Odili and me live a full lifespan. Let us be free again one day."

3

On the morning of the second day, after starting well before dawn, the six canoes rounded a sweeping bend, moving toward a family of hippos. The adults were small, about the size of large goats, the young no bigger than dogs. The young swam behind their parents, the hide above their spinal cords gleaming, eyes and noses just out of water.

Chinwe and Odili, in the third canoe, watched as the hippos swam toward shore and the first canoe swerved. The captain of the slave hunters stood in the bow of the lead canoe and threw his spear. As the spear hit its mark, a ribbon of blood trailed away from a fat young body, and the captain of the slave hunters gave a shout as though, without weapons, he had killed a pair of leopards.

Odili rose up and gave a second shout, an echo of the captain's. The man who paddled the first canoe recovered the body of the hippo and the spear and the six canoes moved off again. They reached a fork, and took the narrower waterway, going under arching mangrove trees, furrowing the darkness of the waters of the river.

A heavy stench came up from the swamp. Ahead lay a circle of bright, hot light which grew ever larger as they slid past the spiderlike roots of the trees. All at once the river widened. The canoes burst into the bright sunlight and the water became a luminescent green. The bottom was gold and just above it Chinwe saw a school of fish, moving as one, darting, knifing toward a stand of grass.

A village stood on a sandspit ahead. Its people launched their small canoes and paddled close to watch them pass. These people, like many others they had passed on the river, were free and unafraid.

For a moment, forgetting her grief, Chinwe was exhilarated. The air on her cheek was a kind she had never felt before, a cool wind bearing a clean and salty smell.

A man walked on the bank of the river, carrying a slim and silvery spear. For a moment she thought he might be her father. But, as he turned to watch the great canoes, she saw that he was not.

Chinwe drew a long breath, viewing the strange and barren land, stripped to its core by wind and sea. A strange white bird, with wings like polished blades, hovered in the sky above the canoes, seeming to let the wind take its body, crying like a cat before it flew across the trees.

As they rounded a final bend in the river, passing a stand of wind-whipped palms, Chinwe's eyes grew wide. Dead ahead, on a sandy hill, stood a cluster of buildings, white as chalk, with golden roofs, one above the other, and lower on the hill were lesser buildings, giving way at last to huts.

As the river curved, the canoes passed the city and headed for a smaller hill, a barren place battered by lines of waves, curling and exploding, sending up towering plumes of white.

Now the canoes were taken by the sea. They mounted the first of the ocean swells and sliced across a second wave.

Some of the captives screamed in fright, but the men at the paddles seemed barely to notice and pointed the bows of the canoes toward a cove, protected by a rock-strewn jetty, a place where the water was flat and still.

The canoes crossed over the gleaming shallows, streaking across the crystal waters, and drove hard up against the beach.

The captain of the fleet was first to disembark. His eyes glittered. His face was flint. Suddenly ugly, he shouted at his captives, his voice like the gibber of a chimpanzee as he scorned, abused and frightened them. His message sullied the beauty of the water, the sun-bleached sand and the city standing against the sky.

The man who had fed them on the bank of the river stood beside his potbellied leader, prodding the captives as they stepped to the beach. He glanced at Chinwe as if at a stranger.

Odili, unmoved by the shouting and prodding, looked in wonder at the city, at the hill in front of it, at the sea. He caught his breath and pressed Chinwe's hand, whispering, "Chinwe. A king!"

A man with skin as black as night came across the crest of the nearest dune. His head was swathed in cloths and feathers, all trailing away along his spine. His arms were ringed by golden bands and his neck supported an expanse of metal, pounded into a flat, bejeweled plate that lay across his chest. He wore a pair of clean white breeches and a flashing red sash. Though he was old and not tall, he gave the impression of having great force. The king's attendants were at his side and behind him followed a column of soldiers carrying muskets, pistols and swords. The tallest of these was clearly their leader, a man with a long, snakelike neck, who was armed with nothing but a knife at his belt. Behind the white-clad men came others, wearing loincloths, carrying spears.

The king stood on a rise and his slaves stood behind him as he waited for the leader of the hunters to approach him. His hips were wide and his navel, below the flat metal plate, protruded like a second, smaller nose.

The two men cracked their fingers in greeting and the king gestured toward the people in chains. The leader of the slave hunters pointed proudly to the best of the men. The king then pointed to the women and laughed and the other laughed with him.

The captors, shouting insults and joking, marched their prisoners up the hill. Chinwe, squinting into the sun, saw that they were trapped, on an island set apart from the city, bounded by the river and a mangrove swamp. On the side of a hill stood circular stockades, their walls made of stakes driven into the earth and lashed together with thin, stout ropes. In front of the compounds lay a stretch of pounded earth and above it, on the crest of the hill, stood the trunks of two palms, sunk into the ground. Near their tops they were crossed by the short, stout trunk of a third, which completed a kind of gallows frame.

A cluster of women, brought here several days ago, stood on the stretch of ground in front of the compounds, dry now in this driest of seasons, much like a marketplace. One woman greeted the· new arrivals, speaking the language of Chinwe and her people.

The king turned to the man with the snakelike neck, calling him Nwoye. Nwoye made the captives stand in lines. He and the others went into a stockade and brought out still more captive men, most of them little more than boys, all chained together by their necks. Many were manacled.

The king was no longer in a mood for jokes. He spoke again to Nwoye, who took out a short knife and moved from one man to the next, cutting off loincloths, amulets and fetishes, leaving the prisoners altogether naked.

As she watched, Chinwe took off her shell, slowly so as not to draw attention to herself, and held it hidden in the palm of her hand.

As Nwoye left the men and approached the women, his manner was respectful. When he came to Chinwe, he cut away the cloth around her hips, examined her earrings, looked into her eyes and moved along.

When he finished stripping the women, he and his servants removed their chains. He said, "Now you can tend your children and cook, as the women who arrived before have done." He motioned toward the mangrove trees. "The swamp devours people," he said. "The river is alive with crocodiles and sharks. The sea, as you can see, is wild."

4

Chinwe looked for her friend Ifeoma and found her sitting alone, dejected. Chinwe encouraged her to rise.

Now Odili was free, he began to play. He drew a circle in the sand, looking up, watching a boy pull another boy down. The boys began to wrestle. They rolled and struck against Nwoye's ankles, and Chinwe, afraid that Nwoye might take them away, held them by their necks and pushed them firmly toward their mothers. Failing to understand Chinwe's motive, both mothers frowned.

Nwoye turned to Chinwe. "I see you have a way with children. Tell the mothers if the children are a nuisance I will pen them in one of the compounds there."

Idoto whispered, "Why do you try to please this man?"

Another woman nodded, as if to ask the question again.

Chinwe stood straight, glancing at Idoto, looking into the other women's eyes. "Surely you can see the reason. If the boys misbehave he will take them away."

Working slowly, Nwoye and his men washed the bodies of the captives, using sponges and water from large copper vessels. One of Nwoye's men washed Chinwe, laughing and making jokes about her body and finally discovering the shell in her hand. Nwoye, overhearing the insults, spoke sharply to the man. "Treat the women with kindness," he said.

"This woman wants to keep a fetish. The shell is worthless, but our king has told us to strip them of their belongings."

Nwoye said firmly, "Let the woman keep her shell."

When the washing was finished, Nwoye's servants rubbed oil on the bodies of the captives. The king, giving special attention to the women, began to strut like a cockerel, his jellylike buttocks doing a dance. However, he never moved in close. He only pointed and spoke to Nwoye and then retired to a large cabana which stood on the opposite side of the hill.

Nwoye showed Chinwe three copper kettles, suspended on poles above a stack of dried wood. Beside the kettles were wooden bowls of uncooked rice. Nwoye showed her a well where they could draw fresh water and pointed to a trench at the bottom of the hill, near the mangrove swamp, where the captives could go to relieve themselves. "Tell the women the time has come to cook," he said.

Chinwe found Ifeoma and, thinking the work might raise her spirits, said, "Idoto and the others have questioned my motives. You are my friend. Will you help me with the cooking?"

Ifeoma said, "Of course." Shyly, she smiled. "Idoto has always been jealous of you."

"Azu is dead. You'd think she might forgive me now."

"Nonetheless, she and some of the others are jealous."

"They know they can trust me. They must know that."

"Like animals in cages, they are naked and afraid."

Ifeoma went with Chinwe to the well and brought back water to fill the kettles. Reluctantly, Idoto and the others followed, helping. The women lit fires underneath the kettles, boiled the water and cooked the rice.

A servant came across the hill, leading a couple of sway-backed horses bearing pouches filled with wooden bowls and crudely fashioned wooden spoons. The bowls and spoons were tied together with cords. Nwoye picked out one of the bowls and looped its cord around his neck, showing the captives how to wear their utensils. Three of his servants handed out the bowls and spoons while Chinwe and the others mixed oil with the rice and served the others and themselves.

After Chinwe had helped feed the people, she walked away from the smoldering fires, stopping on the crest of the hill where she looked out to sea and saw a sailing ship with great white wings, followed by a flight of sea birds. Surely, this wasn't the dreaded ship. The body of the vessel was slim and black, a thing of great beauty, moving relentlessly toward the surf, the lines of white water that broke against the headland. Before the ship reached the breakers, it described an arc, pointing into the wind, her great sails shaking, spilling wind.

Chinwe stood wondering a moment, turned and was face to face with Nwoye. "Is this the ship that will take us away?"

"It is," he said. "She's called the *Maquita.*"

"Are you sure?" she asked. "It seems so small."

Nwoye nodded. "She's built for speed." Studying Chinwe's face, he fumbled for words. "The king is looking for a servant for his house."

Fleetingly, Chinwe saw a chance of escape, perhaps a chance to find her father. Then she remembered the king's appearance. "Would he make me share his bed?" she asked.

57

"Had he wanted a wife, he would have examined the women more closely. His seraglio, on an island close by, is filled with wives and children of the king."

"But I would be his slave, and if he changed his mind, I might become one of his many wives."

"You would indeed be his slave, with little chance of buying your freedom, but if you sail aboard the *Maquita*, you may be one of the ones who dies. If you survive the voyage, the captain will sell you at an auction in Havana. Life for Cuban slaves is hard."

"And what of my brother? Can my brother stay too?"

Nwoye shook his head. "He must go. The king sends many of his children away."

"Will you decide my fate or shall I?"

"You decide," he said.

In giving her a choice, Nwoye had done a special thing. Nevertheless, she said, "Our mother is dead. I must go with my brother."

Nwoye shrugged and turned away.

5

The following morning, an open boat containing three men left the ship and moved across the swells toward the cove. As the boat drew closer, Chinwe saw the sailors clearly. "White men," she breathed.

Odili rushed up to her, pointing toward the headland. The men who had come from the ship climbed the path. The man who appeared to be their captain was stocky. His skin was the color of uncooked beef. He had a flaming, bushy beard and wore a broad-brimmed raffia hat, a brace of pistols and a sword. The other men were young. Both carried muskets. The three men wore an assortment of clothing, breeches and shirts of various colors.

Speaking the language of the captives, the captain of the ship told the men to stand up. He faced the first of them, looking at him closely. "Open your mouth," he said, opening his own.

The man did as he was told and the captain carefully examined his teeth. As the captain touched the man's groin, pushing his finger up toward his belly, the man shrank away but the captain persisted. "Cough," he said.

The man failed to understand and the captain coughed to show him what he wanted.

The man gave an explosive splutter and the captain and the other white men laughed. The captain nodded, repeating the process, then squeezed the captive's arms and legs, testing the soundness of his body.

The captain moved along the column, doing again what he had done to the first, until he stood in front of Obi. Obi kept his lips pressed one against the other, preventing the captain from looking at his teeth.

Nwoye stood above Obi, meeting his eyes. He said, "Open your mouth!"

Obi pushed his lower lip forward, grinding his teeth, making the muscles of his cheeks protrude.

Slowly, Nwoye pulled his knife from its sheath and pointed it toward Obi's groin. "Open your mouth," he said, raising his knife, as if to slash at Obi's flesh.

Slowly, Obi opened his mouth.

As the captain finished with the men, his manner changed. As he moved toward the women, he showed an unexpected shyness.

Nwoye spoke to the women with babies, five in all, telling them to lay their babies on the ground.

A thin young woman with large dark eyes turned a frightened gaze on Nwoye. "Will you take away our babies?"

Nwoye said, "The babies will stay with their mothers."

The captain of the sailing ship scrutinized the first of the women. He passed quickly along the line, barely looking at the bodies of the women, giving most of his attention to their teeth and their eyes. Chinwe stood still as he put his fingertip on her cheek. He examined her eyeballs, one and then the other, as she looked in horror at his skin. It was covered with an intricate pattern of veins, much like the veins of a leaf, but blue. The pores of his nose were large. Wrinkles clawed at his lips, which were revoltingly thin and hard. His eyes were like the eyes of a jungle cat.

When the captain finished his work, the king came forward, the white men approached him and they greeted each other like men who had met before.

The captain started a palaver with the king. Both talked loudly, in a mixture of tongues, waving their arms, pointing and haggling. The captain made marks in a little brown book and spoke to the sailors, who retired to the headland and rowed toward the ship while the captain, slapping the king on his back, retired with him to his cabana.

Nwoye motioned to the captive men to sit. He brought out a box of heavy iron shackles and together with his servants picked out the strongest of the men and bound their ankles, one to the other. Holding one of the pairs of shackles, Nwoye moved toward Obi and knelt at his feet.

Obi stared at the shackles, his lips pulled tight across his teeth. Suddenly he kicked Nwoye's chest. Nwoye lost his balance and toppled but, never seeming to lose his composure, rolled away and rose to his feet. Some of the younger men giggled at Nwoye but he stood his ground, his face revealing no emotion. He knelt again, taunting Obi, waiting for the slightest movement of his body. Pushing close to Obi's face, he struck him with the flat of his hand.

As Obi straightened, blood streamed away from his mouth and Nwoye struck him hard, once more, while two of his servants clapped the irons around his legs.

Angry, silent, Nwoye thrust a set of branding irons into the heart of the nearest fire. He went straight to Chinwe and, staring fiercely into her eyes, spoke in a voice like a small, taut drum. "First I will brand the backs of the men." He clapped the palms of his hands together. "The sharpest pain lasts only a moment." He glanced at the men, then back at Chinwe. "The men will listen to you," he said. "Tell the men they must lie still. Otherwise the branding will cause them great pain. Help me make them understand."

Thinking of his treatment of Obi, Chinwe regarded Nwoye with contempt. "You struck a man who was helpless," she said. "What does it matter to you if you hurt them?"

"I find no pleasure in torturing your people."

"Will you brand the women and children too?"

"We must. You have only to lie on the ground on your bellies."

Chinwe said, "You are beasts."

"This is something I must do."

"Will you mark the babies?"

"The babies will not be branded," he said.

Chinwe raised her chin. Her eyes were bright. "Still, you are a beast," she said.

"Will you help me persuade the men to lie still?" he asked.

"No," she said. "I will not talk for you." She turned to Idoto. "Our men are in chains," she said. "They suffer much indignity. Some men, like Obi, will fight against the branding iron and in doing so will suffer more than necessary. Let us be marked before the men. If the women are brave, the men too will be brave."

Idoto nodded.

Chinwe gazed into Nwoye's face. "Mark me now," she said.

Nwoye turned toward the fire.

Chinwe spoke to her brother. "When he burns me, be silent."

Odili said, "I will turn away."

"Watch and be silent so the men will be silent."

"I will try," said Odili.

Chinwe lay on her stomach, waiting for Nwoye to return from the fire. When she heard his feet, she gathered her fingers into fists and, as the iron bit into the flesh of her back, she shut her eyes and made no sound.

As she waited for the sharpness of the pain to die, she heard the clicking of the chains of the men and the sound of their voices, raised in shame. Obi's voice rose high above the others, reviling the man who held the iron.

As the sharpness of the pain became a sickening throb, Chinwe opened her eyes and, slowly so as not to fall, stood up.

The children looked at Chinwe and some of them began to cry. The other women lay on their stomachs and were branded. The children were held by their mothers and the servants and Nwoye branded them, barely touching their skin and withdrawing. As Odili was branded, his body stiffened but he lay quite still.

Nwoye's face changed as he branded the men. He pressed his lips together hard and drove the iron into the first man's flesh, pushing deep as the man pulled away.

The man beside Obi was thin and docile. As Nwoye branded him, he cried out in pain.

All at once Obi was a man possessed. He rose up squirming, wrenching at his chains and shackles, spitting into Nwoye's face. One of the servants who stood near Nwoye pointed his musket, took aim and fired at the ground between Obi's knees. With the sound of the explosion ringing in his ears, Obi threw his head back and laughed and shouted in defiance.

Nwoye and the tallest and strongest of his servants held Obi down against the ground and Chinwe moved over and stood above them, her arms like rigid poles at her sides, shouting at Obi to stop, to be patient, to save his life and fight again.

As Obi lay still, Nwoye straightened, turning on Chinwe. "Go back to the women. This man is ours."

The servants held Obi while Nwoye took away the chains at his neck and the shackles at his ankles and, with the others, dragged him, screaming, to the brow of the hill.

Nwoye's servants held the lunging, spitting Obi underneath the gallows frame and tied him by his wrists to the crossbeam. Waving the other men away, Nwoye took a whip from one of his servants and, standing with his feet apart, using all the power in his long and graceful body, he brought the lash around and down with a sweeping, slicing motion, flogging, cracking Obi's back.

Obi's body rose and fell with each succeeding blow of the whip. At last he gave a withering shriek and, after the next blow, went limp.

Nwoye threw the whip to the ground, gathered up his shirt and walked toward the fire, facing the deadly stares of the women, the hollow, angry eyes of the men. For a moment he stared into the fire, then, seeming to awaken as if from a trance, looked down at the whiteness of his breeches, spattered and streaked with blood.

Chinwe wanted to curse the man, but knowing he was filled with wrath, knowing he might whip her too, she held back, trembling, putting her arm around her brother, pressing his head against her shoulder.

The sun dipped into the trees beyond the river. Lacerated by the leaves and branches, it filled the sky with Obi's blood.

Three servants went back to where Obi was hanging. Two of them held up his body while the other cut him down.

At first Chinwe thought Obi was dead, but as the soles of his feet touched the earth and settled, he stood, unsteadily at first. Then, supported on either hand, he stumbled toward the other captives, holding his chin up, moving back to the place where the men lay on their bellies.

Chinwe turned to Ifeoma. "It is finished," she said.

"We are slaves," Ifeoma whispered.

Part III
MUTINY

1

It was evening. Nwoye shouted to the women to march.

Chinwe tensed and Odili pressed close to her, holding her hand.

As the column moved down the hill toward the jetty, Nwoye held his lantern high. His mouth was hard. His eyes were cold. All afternoon he had stood above the cargo brought by the sailors from the ship, sniffing at the casks of rum, opening heavy wooden boxes to examine the bright new muskets and pistols.

The moon shone white above the sea. Above the rumble of the surf rose a chorus of drums, sounding in the towering city. It seemed to Chinwe that the drums were talking, sending up a last farewell. Chinwe's heart leaped and the dark fire burning in her soul burst free. Her cry was like the cry of a leopard caught in a trap, and as she voiced her fierce lament, she felt the sting of a lash across her back.

As she turned to face the man who had whipped her, Nwoye told the man to stop.

Chinwe spoke in a clear, strong voice. "I expect no mercy from Nwoye, she said. "Nwoye is the servant of a trader in slaves."

The man raised his whip again, but again Nwoye spoke to him sharply, telling him to stay his hand.

The sailors turned toward the flash of the lantern. Their arms were like tightly woven vines. Their helmsman, wearing dark trousers and a stark white shirt, moved to and fro, singing loudly, slapping gently at the buttocks of the women.

Three open boats rose in the surge behind the jetty.

Four young women who led the column, prodded by the guards and sailors, stepped aboard the closest boat. Chinwe and Odili followed. Odili looked down, judging the distance from the boat to the jetty. He jumped and fell between the boat and the jetty, scraping and damaging one of his legs. He grit his teeth against the pain, but, in spite of himself, he cried out.

Chinwe gave him a hand and with the help of a sailor pulled him back to the jetty again. Odili sat down, nursing his leg, sucking through clenched teeth, breathing hard as Chinwe knelt down and. touched his leg. Odili winced. He said, "No, don't touch it."

Nwoye pushed his lantern close, watching Odili shaking his head, asking where he felt the pain. "Can you walk?" he asked.

Chinwe and Nwoye helped Odili to his feet and Odili hopped a step or two and tried to walk, but the pain was too great. He had to stand on one leg.

Nwoye's face was grave. "This child cannot travel."

Chinwe said, "If he stays, so will I."

Nwoye shook his head. "I picked another woman for the king."

"I know you did. I saw her leave." Going against her anger and her pride, Chinwe begged Nwoye to let her stay. "You showed compassion yesterday. Can you not show compassion today?"

"The king asked for only one woman. Our bargain with the captain of the ship has been struck. We cannot change the head count now."

Chinwe's eyes gleamed in the light of the lantern. Fiercely, she implored Nwoye, "Then you must let him go with me! Your people killed our mother. Now Odili looks to me for protection."

"In order to board the ship, he must climb."

"I will help him board the ship. He is young. I'm sure his leg will mend."

Nwoye spoke to the cocky little helmsman,

speaking the language of the sailors. Then, for the last time, he faced Chinwe. He stood as if he had much to say, as if he wanted to give her a warning, but all he said was, "As you will."

Chinwe and the sailor helped Odili board the boat, the others followed and, as the boat pushed into the dark lagoon, the helmsman shouted to his men. They dipped and feathered their long, thin oars, and in a gathering surge the boat gained speed, plowed into the crests of the waves, soaring upward in sickening leaps, crashing into the darkness of the troughs.

As the vessel crossed the shoal, it bottomed, cracking and groaning before it found water. Then it shot forward, making its way across the sea and coming in under the shadow of the ship, whose great masts stood against the stars.

At last the boat, half full of water and close to swamping, wallowed in the wash of the ship, fended off by wads of hemp. The helmsman and the sailors, like the captives, were frightened, and clutched at a vast net hanging from the rail of ship. They motioned to the women and children to climb up the net to the deck of the ship.

Chinwe's arm encircled Odili's body. She reached with her free hand and stepped to the ladder. Slowly, painfully, they made their way upward, across the dark, rough side of the vessel, Odili using both arms and his one good leg.

Women and children climbed beside them and, directly under them, a woman and her little daughter climbed with the others.

A lantern high above them glimmered at the rail. Chinwe looked down at the mother and daughter. She started to speak, to encourage the woman, and as she did so the child let go and slipped and plunged, without screaming, to the boat below. The climbers froze, looking down, as the helmsman pushed the crumpled body of the child away, letting it slip between the vessels. At first the mother of the child was silent. Then she made choking sounds. She screamed, clinging to the ladder, striking her head against the net, sobbing and yelling, as if to burst the veins of her body. Chinwe said, "You must go on."

The woman, seeming not to hear, called and sobbed until another woman helped her. At last she climbed again, close to Chinwe, and Chinwe and Odili stepped to the deck.

The man who held the lantern was young and his eyes and hair were black as pitch. His cheeks, burned by the sun, were a golden brown. When he saw that Odili was in pain, he motioned to Odili and Chinwe to stand aside while others climbed into the lanternlight.

Chinwe took the hand of the woman who had lost her child, but the woman lunged, as if to throw herself into the sea. Chinwe jumped and held her back, pulling and wrestling, subduing her at last. Then, as Chinwe leaned across the rail, she saw, in the thin, greenish light of the moon, the sailors, jumping free of the boat, clutching at the ladder and climbing. Around the boat the water danced, boiling, racing. Chinwe felt terror as she sensed, then saw, that the water was slashed by the fins of sharks and the foam was dark with the blood of the child.

Chinwe pulled the woman away from the rail and together with Odili they settled on the deck. Now the woman, stunned, sat with her legs pulled tight against her breast and her forehead hard against her knees.

The man with the lantern directed the women coming over the rail to a place that was guarded by a thick-set sailor brandishing a whip. There they clustered, some of them talking, others staring upward into the sky, watching the sailors where they stood along the yards, shouting and shaking out the great white sails.

When the last of the women had boarded the ship, the sailors followed, for the moment leaving the boat where it was.

The man with the lantern spoke to Chinwe, talking in a foreign tongue but clearly asking what had happened to Odili.

Chinwe indicated that his leg was broken.

The man summoned another man, who held

his lantern over Odili. Chinwe studied his face. Like most of the sailors, this man was young. His hair was the color of a field before a harvest and his eyes were as clear and blue as the sea. His face was small and triangular and his skin was deeply pocked and scarred. Talking very slowly in Ibo, he said, "I am a doctor. What happened to your child?"

"The child is my brother. I think the bone of his leg is broken."

The doctor knelt, looking into Odili's face, giving him encouragement. He glanced at Chinwe. "Come with me. Your brother can lean on our arms as we walk."

They moved toward a square of yellow light, in a small house just behind a mast. The doctor passed through a companionway and descended a ladder, holding up his lantern, reaching out to help Odili down. Around them were corridors and doorways. They entered a room which was lit by a lantern, swinging from a beam.

Odili lay down and the doctor pressed his wounded leg, squeezing it just below the knee. He felt the bone and stopped at a small bump, halfway between the knee and the ankle. "I must hurt you," he said. "I will straighten your leg."

Odili, understanding, nodded.

The doctor gripped the leg firmly, above and below the bump, and twisted. Odili writhed in a spasm of pain. The doctor nodded and lifted his lantern, searching through his collection of cures. Chinwe helped him as he bound a piece of wood against Odili's leg, wrapping it tightly with strips of cloth. When he finished, he smiled and said, "Lie still." He turned to Chinwe. "Your brother must rest. I will let him sleep here. You must live below with the women." Fleetingly, without apparent shame, he looked down at her body. He said, "I hope we can find some clothes for the women."

She returned to the ladder and mounted to the deck. The ship was alive and moving now, carried by its billowing sails. Chinwe looked toward shore and saw dozens of tiny spots of yellow, the lights of the city against the blackness of the land. As she watched, the land and the lights seemed to move and grow smaller until the sails slid across them like a curtain and the moon stood high above one of the masts, moving as the ship moved, keeping pace.

2

A couple of sailors lifted and slid away the cover of the place where the women were imprisoned. Chinwe lay on her back, looking up at the square of dark blue sky. A faint touch of early light signaled the coming of another day at sea. Chinwe had counted fourteen days. Under her body, the boards were damp and unforgiving, constantly moving, rising and falling. Her forehead was wet where it rested on her arm. She raised her chin, rolled over and sat against a bulkhead of vertical planks. She looked at the shapes of the women and children, most still sleeping, thinking about her days at sea. The *Maquita*'s cabin boy had died at sea and, needing hands, the fat little cook had picked Chinwe, Ifeoma and three other women to help prepare and serve the food. These five women, only these, had been given cotton garments—brown, sleeve-less, knee-length shirts. This had made Idoto jealous and had made her despise and mistrust the cook. Chinwe didn't trust the cook but he was not a hard master.

Chinwe was facing one of the masts that pierced the deck above her. The mast made straining, creaking sounds, louder than the softer squeals of board against board, the sounds of the confusion of ropes above her, the lines that looked like the web of a monstrous spider.

Across from where she sat was another bulkhead, like the one she leaned against, also fashioned of vertical planks. Beyond it lay the prison where the men were chained.

Except for the times when the men were freed so they could empty their pails and take their food and exercise, they were chained together in twos and fours and then to cables strung across the ship, anchored at their ends to beams. The cables prevented them from using their pails, and the smell of their prison grew stronger by the hour.

During the day the women and children were free to walk the decks amidships, and since there were many fewer women and children than men, the women's prison was big enough for them. The men, however, were tightly packed, some of them sitting against each other.

Obi was clearly the leader of the men. The younger men admired his courage but, thinking of mutiny, Chinwe knew Obi would be a dangerous leader. Surely there were cooler heads among the men.

As she thought without much hope of rebellion, she leaned back hard. The board she leaned against was loose. At first it seemed useless to try to gain entrance to a dark, dank place, probably holding African cargoes—things like coconuts and palm oil—bound for lands across the sea, but soon she began to feel around and after a time she pried away the plank and laid it down. The opening that faced her was tall and thin but still it was wider than her hips. She sat in front of it, concealing it from view, looking upward anxiously. If the sailors did as they had done before, soon they would lower a ladder to the prison and they would see what Chinwe had done. But before she put the plank in place she slid her body into the gap, groping in the darkness, feeling a series of rough wooden boxes, not stacked but resting side by side. The boxes were heavy. They weren't long enough for muskets but they might contain pistols such as the ones the captain wore. Of course they might hold cooking pots, coins or any of a number of other things. She pried away the top of one, felt around and decided it contained at least a few knives. She felt wooden handles and broad hard blades.

She was interrupted by the shout of a sailor.

Frightened, she put her head out and seeing no sailor scrambled out and sat against the gap again, listening, waiting. Then she replaced the plank, fitting its nails back into their holes.

Chinwe was aware that Idoto had been watching. Idoto said, "Why do you pull the ship apart? You will make the sailors angry."

"I am thinking, as I know you are thinking, of revolt. The men will need tools to cut their chains. Some will need weapons."

"What did you find?"

"I found heavy boxes."

Not wanting to talk any more about it, Chinwe reached high, grasped the rim of the hatch and, scrambling and swinging her right leg over, climbed to the deck above. She looked back toward Africa, and saw a tenuous ruffle of clouds, hanging just above the sea. The sun, just rising out of the water, washed away the last two stars.

Chinwe turned toward the sound of a rasping voice and saw the captain next to the helmsman, his red beard gleaming, his arms held high. She sensed that the captain was alarmed at her presence. A young and rough-faced sailor headed toward her, holding a whip at the level of his waist.

Instead of turning her back, Chinwe faced the whip as it grazed her arm, and the sailor raised it high again.

The voice of the captain came again, this time louder than before, and the force of the whip was suddenly broken.

The doctor appeared, moved toward Chinwe and waved the man with the whip aside. He motioned toward the open hatch, toward the hold where the women slept. "You'd better stay below until they put the ladder down."

"The smell below is growing worse."

"We gave the women pails. Do they use their pails?"

"The women keep their prison clean. The men's prison grows worse. Can something be done to help the men?"

The doctor only shook his head. He gave Chinwe a searching look. "I've been wondering what sets you apart from the others. Were you the daugher of a chief?"

"My father was wiser than a chief. He traveled. He studied. Chiefs listened when my father talked."

The doctor glanced toward the vast hatch cover, over the prison of the men. The heavy construction, forming a latticework of wood, was taken off only when the men came up. The doctor asked, "Is your father on board?"

She shook her head. "I don't know where my father is." She pressed her hand against her arm, aware that the whip had cut her flesh.

The doctor saw the wound and said, "Come with me. I will take care of your arm."

Chinwe asked, "Why do you work aboard a ship like this?"

"When I first signed on, I didn't know she carried slaves. God knows why I've stayed aboard." He frowned. "You're better off aboard this ship than most. Most captains think of Africans as cattle. Many let their sailors use the bodies of the women." He paused, tapping his foot against the deck. "Soon this ship will stink like a trench, but alongside any other slaver, it will smell like all the flowers of the forest."

They went to cabin where Odili was sleeping. As the doctor smeared her arm with ointment, Chinwe glanced at her brother. His eyes were shut. His breathing was steady. However evil these people might be, they had been kind to Odili.

Pointing to the place where Chinwe had been branded, the doctor asked, "Has your burn healed as it should?"

Chinwe raised her cotton shirt and the doctor oiled her back. "Your skin is fine."

Odili stirred. Even in the innocence of sleep, his face bore signs of developing manhood, the beginnings of a toughness, tempered, like his father's, by a restless mind. Chinwe wondered what lay ahead for them. Almost as if he had read her mind, the doctor said, "I hope you can live and work together, at least while he is still a boy."

"I must keep my brother with me."

"You might be sold to different men."

Again, the loss of freedom became a burning, weakening fear. "I suppose we might."

As she watched him, Odili opened his eyes.

"Good morning, Odili. How are you feeling?"

"Fine, Chinwe." He worked himself into a sitting position, grasped a loop of rope above his head. "The doctor makes me exercise."

"So would I if I were taking care of you."

The doctor went back on deck with Chinwe. "You can help your brother exercise. I want him to walk on his one good leg. Now the ship is jumping a little. Better to wait until the sea is flat."

"Will he walk and run as he did before?"

The doctor smiled. "He will. I'm sure." His smile disappeared. "He'll probably be running by the time we dock in Cuba."

"Thank you," she said. "For taking care of Odili."

Abruptly the doctor said, "I suppose you must be thinking of rebellion. Even if your men could overpower us, if they were free, without the captain and the mate the ship would drift until you starved."

"The sun is behind us. We have only to turn the ship and follow the sun to Africa."

The doctor shook his head. "The sun, as you know, moves across the sky. The stars do too."

Thinking of the stars above her village, she nodded. "We would study the sun and the stars," she said.

"Without teachers and charts and many months of study, you couldn't learn to sail this ship. Pedro Silva, the black-haired second mate, is young, but before he ever went to sea he learned the arts of navigation. We steer by the sun and by the stars, but without the wind and the motion of the water, we would not move, we could not steer. If your people captured this ship and swung her bow toward Africa, she would drift as she is going now, toward Cuba."

"How did you sail to Africa then?"

"We came from the north, with the wind and the currents." He traced a circle with his hand. "From Cuba we go north and east again, to Spain, before we sail to Africa."

"I see," she said. "We cannot go back."

"Not directly," he said.

"I think you could tell me much, much more."

"Cook will tell you more. Cook's mother, as you know, was Ibo. He speaks your tongue as no white man can speak it, and Cook has spent many years at sea."

3

Later that day, when the cooking was finished, Chinwe and the others stood on deck, beside the cook, near the brick enclosure that held the giant copper caldron in which the food for the prisoners was cooked, filling the serving bowls with rice mixed with oil and boiled potatoes.

The captain stood, as he often did, close to his helmsman, sharp and watchful, as the men began to come up from their prison. The day was hot and the smell came up in sickening waves, striking at the nerves and stomachs of the women, of the sailors who stood around brandishing their whips, slapping at the sheaths that held their knives.

Chinwe felt that there were times when she was close to losing hope, but always something raised her spirits. Now she saw the doctor lifting Odili to the deck, helping him seat himself against the house. Chinwe nodded and smiled at Odili, turned and went about her work, dishing food into the bowls of the men. Some of the men were like death itself, emaciated, dry, their eyes like cavernous, lifeless pits. Others showed spirit, though their bodies were filthy. Some were covered with running sores. Others had bled from fighting their shackles. One came up from the prison alone, dragging the end of a chain and soon thereafter a couple of sailors brought up the body of his partner, one of many men who had died at sea, took it to the rail and threw it over.

Chinwe approached the man whose partner had died, offering food, but he sat down abruptly, curled up in grief, making his body as small as he could. Chinwe spoke as she might have spoken to a child. "It is better to live than to die," she said. "Unless you move, the sailors will whip you. Stand up now and take this food."

The man sat as before and soon a sailor saw him and kicked him. When the kick accomplished nothing, the sailor whipped him. The doctor, seeing what the sailor was doing, made him stop. The doctor took the wrist of the captive and, exhibiting unexpected strength, pulled him up until he was standing. Then he moved among the others, cleansing their sores, smearing them with ointment.

Chinwe drifted toward her brother, who stared at the place where the sailors had jettisoned the dead man's body. Chinwe said, "Odili?"

"What is it?"

"This voyage will not go on forever. The doctor says it will end in a month, but before it ends, more men will die."

"Why are so many sick, Chinwe?"

"They lie together like fish in a basket, chained to a cable and to each other. The spirits of most of them are low. Some of them simply want to die."

"Will we ever go home?"

"I hope so, Odili."

"If we do, do you think we can find our father?"

"Yes, though it might take many months. Father is known throughout our land and many other lands as well."

Aware that the captain's eyes were on her, Chinwe moved away from Odili, took up a heavy jug of water and filled it from one of the casks on deck. Other casks, she knew, were stored below. Cook had said, that although there was an ample supply of water, they must give it out slowly so that if the ship was delayed at sea by a lack of wind or by a storm the supply would last until it reached land.

Obi hadn't come up on deck and Chinwe began to wonder if he might be sick. He might have died. Of course she didn't wish him dead, but Obi was a danger. If Chinwe had indeed found weapons for the men, she thought she saw how they might take over the ship. But Obi, in his mindless rage, would want to make their rising a slaughter.

How foolish to wonder if Obi might be dead. As Chinwe began to serve the food, he climbed the ladder, bright-eyed and strong, almost dragging the man he was chained to, a thin man, little more than a boy. If only Obi's intelligence equaled his strength! Chinwe wished with all her heart that Azu were living, that Azu stood now in Obi's place.

Obi glanced at Chinwe and turned away, scanning the deck, glancing at a sailor who stood by the anchor winch, eyeing the helmsman who spun the wheel gently as the ship breasted one of a series of swells, and the captain standing beside him, talking. He fingered his wooden spoon and bowl, glancing at the cook, who was sweating profusely and wiping his forehead with a dirty white cloth.

As Chinwe passed food to the second batch of men, she lingered with some of them, giving them comfort. As she moved toward Obi, he avoided her eyes, looking into the bottom of his bowl.

"Are you crazy?" she asked. "How can you harden your heart against me?"

"After they whipped me, you spoke to our captors. During these sickening days at sea you've sucked at the teats of the half-breed cook."

"Obi, you are the world's worst fool. You rebel

against your fate with the cunning of a child who rebels against his parents. Like you, I don't quite trust the cook, but working for him gives me freedom."

"Never speak to me again."

"I will speak when I wish to, to you above others. Your every move and every look has signaled what you hope to do. You want to free yourself, to kill. Surely you can see that you must hide your intentions."

Looking down at a link of chain at his ankle, Chinwe saw a rough bright spot. "I see you are working to free yourself. Good. Conceal your work and mask your anger. Make them think your spirit is broken."

She rolled a ball of rice and meat between her palms and dropped it into Obi's bowl.

"I have nothing more to say," he told her.

"I have much to say to you." She glanced at the boy who was shackled to Obi. As she gave him his food, the boy looked up at her, gratefully. Chinwe asked Obi, "What is your plan?"

"After I free myself, I will free the others. The strongest of us will rise and kill."

"A plan as spare as that will fail."

"Anything is better than living in chains."

"I may have found weapons. If so, I think I have a plan."

"Where are the weapons?"

The doctor, who was washing the backs of the men, was moving closer. Chinwe said, "We'd better talk another time."

When the feeding was finished, Chinwe sat against the house with Odili and some of the other women and children, watching as the sailors made the prisoners move. Chinwe caught her breath as the man who had been chained to the man who had died stared wildly, madly, into the sky, leered at the others and started for the rail. One of the sailors, seeing what he was doing, raised his whip and struck the man a vicious blow. The man sprawled, helpless, on the deck.

Some days a red-haired, red-faced mate played a white man's fiddle and the sailors made the prisoners hop and dance. Always the prisoners were whipped, not for doing something wrong, but simply to keep their bodies in motion. Today the fiddler appeared with a drummer. The fiddler stood aside. The sailor holding the drum was large. He squatted, facing a knot of prisoners, and smiled, displaying his yellow teeth. The prisoners, most of them young, were frightened. All began to hop. The sailor raised his chin and laughed. "*Mak Mumbo!*" he said. *Mak Mumbo* meant nothing, but he laughed again, setting down the drum near a big-eyed youth, tapping the hide of the drum with his knuckles. The sailor's play made the young man smile, and when he saw he wouldn't be whipped, he pulled the drum toward himself and, using his free hand, tapped out a series of short, quick sounds. The man he was chained to moved his body with the beat and, using his free hand, touched the drum. Soon they were drumming as one and laughing, making the others relax and smile.

Now some of the captives who had hopped in fear began to move their bodies in a dance. But then, suddenly aware of the sadness of the dancing, the drummer made an angry face and, holding his hands high, bringing them down hard, drummed a familiar song of war, a rising fiery jungle sound.

At first the sailors stood as if stunned, then fear flickered in their eyes and their whips came into play. Not quite wanting to whip the drummer, they flicked their whips at the ankles of the dancers and the dance became a parody, a nightmare vision.

Chinwe looked for Obi who, having taken her warning, shuffled dumbly with his partner. As she had done many times since the burning of her village, Chinwe remembered the celebrations. And now, watching the men as they moved in sickness and in shame, she knew that if she had to she would kill to escape, to run, to be free.

4

Six days later, in the afternoon, as Chinwe and Cook were working on deck, the lookout above them began to shout. Chinwe leaned back and bent her neck, gazing at the man aloft, who pointed toward a yellowish cloud, dead ahead, just above the horizon. The men were firmly locked in their prison while the women and children moved on deck, some of the children playing together, others clinging to their mothers.

Chinwe asked Cook why the lookout had shouted.

"Line squall coming. We'll soon be sailing in heavy seas. Hurry! Help me tie things down."

Already the sky was a mass of clouds. Ahead, where the lemon-colored cloud had been, sea met sky in a smoky blur. The captain appeared, his hair in a tangle, squinting at the vessel's bow as it sent up towering bursts of white. A whistle sounded, shrill and insistent. The sound was bringing sailors on deck. As he shouted his orders, the captain was a man of rock and iron.

His arms and hands moved in encompassing signals as he gestured toward the sails and the ratlines.

Chinwe helped Cook wrestle with a hose to douse the fire under the big copper caldron, Chinwe holding the hose while the cook pumped water. The coals hissed and spat and at last went dead.

Some of the sailors, responding to the whistle and the voice of the captain, swarmed up the ratlines, gathering and furling the sails while a couple of older ones worked on deck, herding the women into their prison, preparing to close it.

Chinwe and Cook gathered the smaller pots and stowed them in a box that was lashed to a mast. Already the wind was picking up sharply, screeching in the rigging. Above the sounds the ship was making came the scream of a woman.

Chinwe stepped toward her and took her by the wrist, but one of the sailors pushed Chinwe aside and drove the woman to the top of the ladder. The woman looked wildly around the deck, toward the sea where it came across the bow, where it ran along the deck. "My child!" she screamed. "My child is lost!"

The woman might simply be demented but, giving her comfort, Chinwe called to her, "I'll look for your child."

Another sailor pushed Chinwe toward the

ladder but she pounced on a coil of rope near Cook, picking at it, pretending to help him. "Please," Chinwe implored. "Tell the sailors you need me."

"Why do you want to stay on deck?"

"I want to look for the woman's child. I want to be near my brother in the storm."

Whip in hand, a sailor was moving toward Chinwe, but Cook spoke to him sharply and the sailor shrugged, moved away and helped the others cover the prison where the women and children huddled together, waiting for the storm to strike. Despite her mistrust of him, Chinwe was grateful to Cook.

The sailors aloft, who had taken in sail, scrambled down the tar-soaked shrouds.

Working feverishly with Cook, Chinwe scanned the deck, looking for the child. The woman must have been wrong. The child must have climbed down before her and by now was probably safe below.

Looking at the sky again, Cook said, "The wind is still rising. Soon even the sailors will go below, leaving only the men at the helm." Cook took her hand and, clinging to each other, finding handholds as they went, they traversed the deck, running into sheets of spray, going toward the house. A flood of water crossed the deck, and as she watched it blacken the boards, she felt a sense of dread, turned away for a moment from the cook and, almost as if she had conjured up an image, a child appeared, a little girl, clinging to a coil of rope at a mast, letting go, sliding, slowly at first, going against the grain of the deck, tumbling toward the dark green sea.

Chinwe broke away from Cook and made a long dash toward the rail. As the bow rose, the motion of the ship stopped the progress of the child. The deck gave a great convulsive shudder as it dropped again toward the mad white sea and the child slid once again toward the rail and caught in the scuppers, giving Chinwe a chance to reach her and grab her wrist before the deck rose up again. In her terror, the little girl was gibbering and calling, but the sound of her voice was lost in the wind.

Chinwe, clinging to the child and clutching the rail, felt her strength begin to drain. She cried against the power of the sea, stared wildly toward the house. Cook stood in the companionway, staring at her as he might have stared at a corpse. He made no move to help her. Behind him, the captain, alone at the helm, was rooted firmly to the deck, squinting across the wild, white water.

Pedro Silva pushed past the cook and, braving the monstrous convulsions of the deck, made his way forward toward the base of a mast, clinging, crawling, as he went. He grasped the end of a rope, looped it around himself, knotted it and, moving as a monkey might scramble down a vine, lowered and clawed his way toward the rail where Chinwe and the child were perched, now awash, now lifted, soaking, toward the sky. A huge wave moved toward the ship, followed by a gash of pure white spume.

Chinwe closed her grip on the wrist of the child, the mate took one of his hands off the rope and, using his free arm, encircled Chinwe. Sliding his arm around her waist, he reached and gripped the rope again. Now, using both hands, he worked them slowly toward the mast.

Chinwe, feeling the roughness of the rope against her shirt, told the child to hold fast to the garment. Then she pulled her to the base of the mast where they rested a moment, gazing out at the fury of the sea, at the feathery crowns blowing off the waves, flying as a white mist high above the troughs.

Resting a moment, the mate breathed hard, looked at Chinwe as if to ask a question. But instead he simply pointed to the house.

Chinwe held her hand up, a signal she wanted to rest a moment longer. The child held fast, quivering, silent, until without warning, at a moment when the deck was more or less level, she wrenched away and scrambled toward the hatch above her mother's prison. Chinwe reached out, but not in time, and the child was swept away again.

Pedro Silva motioned to Chinwe to stay where

she was and again he made a journey across the deck. But before he could reach the helpless child, a wave came aboard, its waters shattered, coursed across the deck, lifted the child and swept her into the sea.

Silva lay motionless on the deck, clinging to his lifeline, watching the place where the child had disappeared. He turned his face toward the captain, then toward Chinwe and pulled himself hand over hand to the mast.

Sitting beside this white-skinned man, she moved her hand and touched his wrist, thanking him as best she could for saving her from drowning, for doing his best to save the child. Then, above the roar of the wind, the scream of the ribs and boards of the ship, the bone and flesh of this hellish vessel, she heard a sound that made her let go of Silva's wrist, cringe and tighten the muscles of her belly. She heard a chorus of screams and the pounding of chains, the sounds of the raging of the men in their prison. Then the thing they were learning to live with came stronger than ever, this time carried on a blast of wind, the smell of the people imprisoned below, the sickening stench of vomit and offal. And, responding to the sounds and smell of this place, Chinwe made fists and shut her eyes. Again she felt the touch of the mate and he led her away from the mast to the house.

5

Next morning the sea was a great savannah, a flat and friendly field of blue. The smells of the *Maquita* hung hot above her shrouds and drifted many miles to leeward.

Chinwe decided to investigate the boxes. Working fast, she removed the board, crept in, and one by one pried them open. Two contained bush knives, coated with oil, long and lethal instruments, used for cutting sugarcane. They were twelve to a box, wrapped in cloth and packed in paper. Other boxes contained brass fittings which appeared to have something to do with the ship.

She returned to the women's prison, replaced the board, waited for the sailors to put down the ladder and went, as she always did, to the galley, to help the cook serve food to the sailors.

The memory of Cook's face in the storm, his willingness to watch her die, to watch as she and the child were drowned, without so much as moving a muscle, had spread like poison to her heart. The vision of that pale, brown face, African features, dark eyes watching, had come to her again and again last night.

Cook served bowls of cereal to the crew, and Chinwe took a tray to the captain's cabin, a tray bearing cereal, two slices of bread, an orange and a pot of tea. The motion of the ship was gentle. She balanced the captain's tray with ease, stepping lightly with the motion of the deck.

On days like this, when the wind was light and the stench of the prisons soaked every board and nail of the ship, when the only escape was into the shark-infested sea, the captain lapsed into dark and bitter silence. Now, after the storm, after the heroism of his mate, Chinwe hoped that he would speak. Most days he presented an impenetrable wall, giving no sign that he knew of her presence.

She stood in front of the door and knocked.

"Enter!" he bellowed.

She paused a moment on the threshold. The captain stood with his back to Chinwe, looking through a porthole, staring at the sea.

The captain's chair was made of mahogany, polished and bearing a velvety cushion. All the walls were polished too, and a fine bright lamp swung overhead. Chinwe put the tray down in front of the chair and, following the captain's gaze, saw two small birds above the sea, diving, soaring, flitting across the tops of the waves. The captain turned abruptly, retreated to his table and, never looking into her face, spoke in Ibo but as if to himself. "Those birds are one of the mysteries of the sea. I've seen them a thousand miles from land. I've never seen them rest or sleep. Some say they bring trouble." His laugh was brittle. "We've just had a storm. Maybe now we'll have another kind of trouble." At last he faced her. "God knows why you're still alive."

"Because of the mate."

"If Pedro Silva had lost his life saving a foolish Ibo slave, I might have thrown that slave to the sharks."

"Pedro Silva saved a woman, not a slave."

"I see you're a troublemaker," he said. "I'm a fool to give you the run of the ship."

As she was leaving, Chinwe said, "Surely you have nothing to fear from a woman."

As she left the captain's cabin and climbed to the deck, Chinwe heard screams coming up from below. When the screaming stopped, the men began to struggle up the ladder, blinking into the light of day. One of the younger men was sobbing and when Chinwe spoke to him, giving him comfort, he only retched and turned away. Soon the cause of his distress was apparent. Two big sailors climbed the ladder, dragging Obi with them. Obi's back was cut and bleeding. A length of severed chain clung to his wrist. He was wild with rage.

Obi's partner came up like a lamb, behind a third sailor, and sat beside Obi, waiting for someone to fill his bowl.

As Chinwe served Obi, he stared at the deck.

His partner trembled as he spoke. "We are finished," he said.

Chinwe looked down at Obi's head. "I warned you about your chains," she whispered. "Now, as I speak to you, I beg you to listen. I found two boxes of knives in the hold. Striking one knife against the other, you can roughen their edges and use them to cut the links of your chains." She slapped her foot against the deck. "First you must loosen the planks between our prisons."

"We have tried and failed. They never chain me in the same place twice."

Chinwe gave Obi's partner his food. "I have a plan. Trust me. Whenever you can, spend your efforts on the plank. Work at night. Conceal your efforts."

"Why should we trust you?"

"You must. If you do another foolish thing, if you threaten the safety of the ship and our people, if the sailors don't kill you it is I who will drive a knife into your back."

Obi was stunned. As Chinwe moved away feeding and talking to the others, she knew he was watching her, taking her measure in a way he never had before.

Cook, as always, was pleasant. As Chinwe and

the other women finished the feeding, he said, "I suppose the man Obi has given up hope."

Mistrusting Cook, she said, "Now he will never escape and he knows it."

All at once, watching Cook's face as he spoke, Chinwe knew he was a spy. She should have known it long ago. Speaking Ibo as he did, he listened. She had seen him several times talking to the captain. Chinwe was suddenly, fiercely, proud. How sad to be a mixture of peoples. How sad to split one's loyalties.

She took up a container of water and began, as did Ifeoma and the others, to circulate among the men, pouring water into their bowls. Not knowing Chinwe hoped to speak to Obi again, Ifeoma moved toward him and gave him his ration of water. One bowl each two times a day was all the captives were allowed, unless a prisoner was clearly sick. Chinwe knew that without an excuse she had better not speak to Obi again. Maybe it was just as well. The captain and cook had seen them talking too often.

Chinwe knelt in front of a dejected man, someone she'd never noticed before. The man's eyes held only a flicker of life. Chinwe filled his bowl. "Speak," she said.

His voice was thin. "Obi expects us to rise," he said. "If we do, they will whip us."

"If the rising is successful, we will cut your chains. After that you can sleep on deck."

He shook his head. "I only want to die," he said.

Attuned to sounds that might mean danger, Chinwe heard Idoto's voice rise above the others. She wheeled and saw Idoto quarreling with Obi. She caught no more than a word or two but gathered that Obi, despite his anger, had told Idoto to follow Chinwe. Idoto was refusing, questioning Chinwe's right to lead.

Chinwe said angrily, loud enough for Cook to hear, "What foolish talk! The men are in chains. The women must bend to the will of their masters."

Obi retired and others were brought up from the prison. Chinwe took up a bowl of potatoes and glanced again for a moment at the sea. There were the birds of trouble again. One of them dropped and touched the water, rising instantly again, bearing an invisible prize. Under her breath Chinwe repeated, "Trouble." Her plan for mutiny was sound, as good as any, but the ground ahead was littered with traps. Idoto was openly hostile now. It was almost funny, watching her spread her special poison. True, Ifeoma had a following too. Many of the sick, the weak, and the spiritless looked to Chinwe and Ifeoma for comfort and hope as they clung to life, but Chinwe would need the connivance and aid of the strong. Obi, of course, posed the greatest danger. Chinwe must talk again to Obi.

6

Chinwe awakened. Something had touched her.

All night she had heard insistent sounds like the constant gnawing of an army of rats—the sounds of Obi, his partner and others, working to free a plank. She had slept only lightly until an hour or so ago, when fatigue had at last sent her reeling into dreams.

Now the touch came again and, groping in the darkness, she grasped a hand. Now fully awake, she rose to a sitting position. A wide plank next to her shoulder was missing. Before she began to form her words, she choked on a draft of fetid air. Then, above the sounds of passage, Chinwe's voice rose in a hard dry whisper. "Obi, is it you?"

"Give us the knives!" Obi said breathlessly.

Chinwe spoke sharply. "First we talk. I know the ship well. I've worked with Cook and listened to the doctor."

"I despise the cook. The cook is a chameleon."

Chinwe said, "Worse. The cook is a spy." She leaned toward Obi. "The cook is a liar but the doctor is truthful. The doctor has taught me many things. If we conquer the sailors, whichever way we point this ship the motion of the wind will take us away from home, toward Cuba. The currents, like the winds, go west. Without first sailing north, the captain himself couldn't take us back home."

"The doctor lies as does the cook."

Chinwe continued. "If we make the food and water last, or find a way to take on more, we can sail a great circle, with the wind and the currents, and at last reach home. But without the knowledge of the captain or the black-haired mate we would wander like sightless people in a jungle, wasting food and water, and one by one we would sicken and die."

Obi said, "I want the knives."

"Daylight is coming. If the sailors find you free again, they will lock you alone in a very small prison and leave you there until you die." She raised her voice. "Are there ten of you strong enough to fight?"

The voice of an older man came from the darkness, deep and steady. "Yes," the man said, "There are ten at least."

Obi said, "At least fifteen."

Now Idoto's voice came out of the darkness. "Why do you follow a woman?" she asked. "This woman is the white man's pet. She is not to be trusted. She let a lost child die in a storm."

Chinwe ignored Idoto. "Time is short. Put the plank back where it belongs. Tonight, as soon as they cover our prison again, I will tap on the wall. Then you can remove the plank. I will pass a couple of knives in then. Roughen them and use them to free yourselves. At least ten men must be ready to fight. We rise before dawn."

"Climbing up from your prison," Obi added.

"Yes. We can slide away the cover. Remember this. Tell all the others. As the mutiny starts, the men remaining below must talk and cry and rattle their chains. They must sound as they sound on every other morning. If the people are silent, the captain will take that silence as a warning."

Idoto said, "If we follow your plan, we will all be killed."

The voice of the older man came again. "The chances of success are small, but even if we fail, the captain won't kill us."

Chinwe said, "You are right. Only the mutineers will suffer. Among the women, only I need risk my life. I will show the men the way."

Obi said, "We need no guide. The whites must die."

Chinwe spoke sharply. "I want to speak to you alone. Reach out your hand and help me in."

Obi did as he was told. As she slid through the opening, she felt his shoulder, his head, his ear.

"Kill only as many men as you must and promise, on the heads of your fathers, that you and the others will spare the doctor and the black-haired mate. The captain might be useful too."

"I refuse to promise to spare the captain."

"All right," she said. "You are a chief. The captain is a chief. Let the two chiefs fight each other. But unless we spare the mate we will fail. The mate knows how to direct this ship. Spare the doctor. The doctor has helped me. He can help us all."

"I cannot promise things like this."

Chinwe heard sailors overhead, probably come to release the women. "Promise." she hissed.

"I promise," he said. "The sailors are coming."

7

There was just enough light, from the last of the moon and from the stars, filtering through the grille above them, so Chinwe could see the shapes of the people, the women and children, huddled together.

Obi came into the women's prison first, hunching, wielding one of the knives. Others followed, leaving the bulk of the men behind.

Chinwe guarded the remaining knives, holding one of them in her hand. Obi faced her, breathing hard.

Idoto said, "Obi—kill them all!"

The blade of Chinwe's knife flashed in the darkness. "Idoto, shut your mouth," she said. She spoke quickly, directly to Obi and the men who gathered at his side. "How many?"

"Fifteen," Obi said. "More will follow."

"Listen," Chinwe ordered him. "Lift and push away the cover, just enough so we can pass. I will go first. Obi, I want you to hold my knife while I climb. If they see me with a knife we're lost. If the deck is clear, I'll take the knife from you. After that the men will follow, Obi first and then the others."

"I'll attack the helmsman first," Obi said.

"No. You follow me. First attack the captain. Follow me across the deck to the house. I know where the captain sleeps. The door to his cabin is probably locked. Together we can break it in."

Obi said, "The others will attack the helmsman."

"They will." Chinwe searched vainly for Obi's face, looked for the glimmer of one of his eyes, but all she saw was the shape of his skull, a dark blob drifting just above his body. "Obi, pick a man who is fast and young to act as a sentry."

"Olaudah here is fast and brave."

When Olaudah came forward, Chinwe told him, "Stay close to the nearest mast—the great pole rising up, just there. Hide in the shadows." She pointed upward. "If a sailor investigates too closely, if he notices the gap between the cover and the deck, attack him as quietly as you can, putting your hand across his mouth. No matter how much you might want to leave it, guard the hatch above this prison. We must keep it open so the others can follow, so we can retreat to our prisons if we must."

Obi said, "It is time to start."

Chinwe swept Obi's impatience aside. "Fourteen men will crawl along the deck, going toward the men at the wheel, seven on one side, seven on the other. Stick like lizards to the rails. The helmsmen watch the sails and the water. Before you attack them, crawl as close as you can. Attack without killing. Fourteen men can overpower two or three. Remember, Obi gave me his promise to spare the doctor and the black-haired mate. If you can, you must capture, not kill, the sailors. We cannot sail this ship alone."

Obi said, "Enough talk. Our men are trained in the ways of war."

The tallest of the people, both men and women, reached up and lifted the cover slowly. The motion of the ship almost made them drop it, but, straining hard, they moved it back, leaving an opening big enough to climb through.

Chinwe stood a moment and listened. The sounds of the ship seemed just as they should be, sailing in a moderate sea, but the prison of the men seemed unnaturally quiet. Chinwe whispered, "Tell the men in the prison to make more noise."

No sooner had she spoken than they heard a sharp, metallic rap, followed by a cry of pain. Chinwe stiffened. A man attempting to sever a chain must have cut himself instead. Chinwe stared upward at the slit of sky, a strip of fine, blue, deep-dyed cloth.

Following the scream came a jumble of talk and pleading, clutching, frightened talk.

A voice, probably that of Pedro Silva, came strong and clear. Chinwe exhaled. "We must wait," she said.

Obi made a guttural sound but waited.

Finally, Chinwe gave Obi her knife. She turned to Olaudah, asking for a boost. As her shoulders cleared the edge of the hatch, she rested, long enough to scan the deck. A single sailor stood on the foredeck, silhouetted against the sky, probably avoiding the smell of the prisons. Back aft, two men stood at the helm. One, she thought, was Pedro Silva.

Chinwe pulled herself up, as she had before, but this time slowly, carefully, keeping low. She stood in the shadow of the mast, stock still. Accustomed to darkness as she was, the night seemed altogether too bright. She scanned the deck, below the rail, where the men would crawl toward the sailors at the wheel. She knelt and reached down for her knife. She waited. "Obi, give me my knife," she said.

"I will lead this mutiny," he replied.

She pushed her face back into the hold. "Give me the knife or I'll finish it now. All I have to do is cry out."

The knife came up. "Now send Olaudah," she said.

As Olaudah followed, Chinwe knelt. Olaudah's eyes, even in the light of night, were bright. Chinwe whispered, "Obi will follow me into the house. As the others come up, please tell them again. They must go slowly, crawling as they would in an ambush in the forest. Give us plenty of time. The sounds of a struggle will awaken the captain."

Obi came up and sat beside Chinwe who asked, "Are you ready?"

"Yes."

They both lay flat as she led him around the hatch and headed toward the house, staying in the shadows, going toward the open companionway. Chinwe motioned to Obi to wait while she went ahead. She ducked into the companionway. Hearing only her brother's and the doctor's steady breathing, she beckoned to Obi to come in. Her heart thumped wildly in her throat. Obi stubbed his toe against a door and Chinwe reached back and took his wrist, leading him toward the captain's cabin. They faced the door and Chinwe whispered, "Now—together. Smash it down."

8

Using their bodies, holding their knives behind their backs, they attacked the door, Obi first, hitting it with his rock-hard body. Chinwe following, throwing her weight against it, making it give way at last.

The cabin was filled with the dim yellow light of a lantern whose wick was turned down low. The captain sat up in his bunk, reached to a shelf and swept up a pistol while Obi flew in all his rage, his arms like wings, enfolding his prey. The pistol cracked. Obi's knife came down, and as it fell, so did Obi, his fluttering arms seeming almost to keep him aloft, then weakening, folding, as his head lolled and slid away like the tail of a snake behind its body, revealing the captain, his beard above a flowing white shirt, blood coming, one hand groping for the shelf again, taking up another pistol.

Chinwe's knife flew across the captain's body, striking the hand that groped for the pistol. The captain gave a bellow of rage. As Chinwe hung above him, his eyes were wild, then he fell back to his bunk and lay still.

As she reached for the captain's second pistol, footfalls pounded overhead. She heard a shot, a cry of death. She found the pistol's hammer cocked, picked up her knife from where it lay across the captain's still, white form and, knife in one hand, pistol in the other, stood behind the splintered door. There she waited, picking out sounds, until she heard her brother's voice. "Chinwe!" he called. "Are you there, Chinwe?"

Above the cry of her brother's voice came footsteps clicking near the door. The man who stepped into the room was the doctor. He stood for an instant, holding a pistol, facing the pulsing white garment of the captain, gazing at the dark and twisted Obi, then he turned and faced Chinwe.

The dim light caught his yellow hair. He didn't flinch or turn away, seemed not to hear the sounds on deck. He seemed suspended, as if in a state between sleeping and waking. Staring steadily into her face, he lowered his pistol. Chinwe trembled but she moved away, letting her knife hang loose in her hand, pointing her pistol at the knees of the doctor. Halfheartedly, the doctor blocked her way with his body but Chinwe pushed past him, going toward the door.

"If you must go, leave your weapons behind. The ship is swarming with men who will kill you."

Chinwe spoke fast. "I intend to join the men in the fighting."

Odili cried out again, this time louder than before, his voice rising high above the sounds of battle. The doctor turned to examine the captain and Chinwe ducked out, groping toward the doctor's cabin. As she reached its door, she saw that the companionway was open. Already, the light of day came in.

She entered the doctor's cabin, setting the knife down on a chair, keeping her pistol in her hand, and quietly closed the door behind her. "Odili," she said. "You must not cry out."

"Stay with me, Chinwe. The sailors will kill you."

As Odili spoke, the door flew open. Pistol in hand, Chinwe spun and faced the cook, who flashed a cleaver, much like the bush knives the mutineers were using. Cook sprung at Chinwe holding his arm high, aiming at her neck. She fired her pistol, hitting him low on the bib of his apron. Cook's arm dropped, his cleaver clattered to his feet, he tilted slowly toward Chinwe and fell against her body, knocking her backward, pinning her against her brother's bunk. She dropped the pistol, embracing his body. The ship gave a lurch and he slid away, crumpling, thudding at her feet.

Cook lay still. "Chinwe, are you hurt?" Odili asked.

She stood, unsteadily at first, putting the back of her hand against her head. The room did a half spin, paused and came back. Chinwe sat against Odili's bunk.

Odili took her by the hand. "Do you think the men have captured the ship?"

Chinwe cocked an ear toward the door. The firing had stopped. A single cry, coming from the deck above, echoed in the corridor. As she listened, the doctor passed, paused a moment and glanced into the room. He was apparently headed toward the ladder to the deck.

Cook, a dark shape at her feet, made a high-pitched wheezing sound. Odili, frightened, said, "The cook is still alive!"

Chinwe spoke softly. "He cannot be alive." Again the room spun and spun, but in spite of her dizziness, she stumbled toward the door, toward the morning light slanting away from the sky. Holding the door frame tightly with one hand, leaving the bush knife on the chair, she stood against the pitching of the ship, stepped up the ladder toward the deck. Cautiously, she raised her head. The ship was sailing as before. She put a foot on deck and raised her eyes above the level of the house. It was then that she saw the litter of bodies, Africans and others, at the side of the house, and dark blood soaking into the deck. Three Africans, very much alive, stood behind Pedro Silva and the helmsman. One was Olaudah, who had acted as sentry, and the other, an older man who seemed to have taken command of the ship, held a musket at the back of the mate. Many more Africans must have escaped. They ranged the deck, some unarmed, others armed with knives or pistols. Three guarded a group of sailors who sat on deck, eyes empty in defeat. The arm of one was streaked with blood and the doctor knelt beside him, calling him by name, twisting a cloth around his arm, just under his shoulder.

Chinwe stepped over the bodies of the dead, toward the men at the helm. Pedro Silva's face was gaunt. As he watched her advance, his mouth became a thin, hard line.

The doctor, pushing back his cornsilk hair, moved among the dead and dying, attending Africans and sailors alike. He stopped beside a coil of rope, picked up a pistol from the deck and with a vicious flick of his wrist threw it into the sea.

The man who seemed to be the leader approached Chinwe, nodding. "Your plan was a good one. We took the ship." He searched her face. "The doctor says Obi and the captain are dead."

Slowly, speaking almost as a child, Chinwe asked, "What is your name? The ship is yours."

"My name is Okara."

Speaking as if each word brought pain, Chinwe said, "Tell the men the killing is finished. Watch the woman called Idoto. Idoto is sour. She might cause trouble."

Okara said, "The killing is finished."

Chinwe nodded, turning away, walking toward the bow of the ship. She, who had seemed the toughest of the women, tougher than many of the men, slumped against a mast, desolate, despairing, and scanned the sea.

Part IV
A LAND APART

I

Ten days after the rising of the slaves, shortly after the sun reached its zenith, Chinwe stood with Odili, watching a line of trees slide by. The *Maquita* was sailing in a narrow channel, with islands of various sizes around her. Though plowed fields lay behind the trees, they had seen no people.

Everyone on board was on deck, lining the rails, staring at the New World, guessing what it held for them, freedom or bondage, life or death.

The ship sailed in a gentle breeze, approaching a broad expanse of shallows, rippling green below the ship. A storm had blown them close to shore and yesterday morning they had seen the first of the large white gulls much like the birds at the mouth of the Niger, a sign that land was not far off.

Odili, walking with confidence now but still not able to run as he had, stopped and pressed against a rail, looking downward, watching a school of porpoises, jumping, gleaming at the bow of the ship.

Chinwe left Odili and moved back along the deck. The dead had long ago been buried at sea and the Africans, together with some of the sailors, had scrubbed the prisons. Now it was the sailors who were kept below.

Chinwe had talked to Okara and the others about their course and destination. It seemed they had, long ago, left Cuba behind them. Until the storm, Okara had been convinced that they were sailing a course that would, in time, take them back to Africa but now it looked as if Silva had lied. The trouble was, Okara had no way of knowing. Serious problems faced them now. Only six casks of water were left. Rice and meat were in short supply. Many experienced sailors were dead and, because there were only a few skilled hands, some of the sails had been badly torn.

Pedro Silva shouted to a sailor who threw a lead line over the side, pulled it up again and called out the depth of the water.

Suddenly, the ship gave a monstrous lurch and the wheel spun, like a thing gone mad, almost breaking the helmsman's arm. Silva gave another shout and three of the sailors climbed high to a yard and began to furl the largest sail.

Odili watched the porpoises frolic away and disappear. He made his way back along the rail, stood with his sister and examined the land.

Chinwe asked the doctor, who stood close by, "How long will this delay us?"

"Silva says we're stuck until morning." As he spoke, Chinwe looked into the gray and twisted trees which were hung with a kind of bluish moss, trailing away like dancing skirts, stirring in the soft, light airs, deepening the shadows at the roots of the trees.

All at once, an African appeared, staring fixedly at the ship. It was then that Chinwe began to look closely, discovering many clusters of people, all black, peering at them from the shelter of the moss. All were unarmed, carrying no firearms, spears or knives, and soon, with a sinking of the heart, Chinwe saw the reason why. Five white men, with sunburned skins, carrying muskets, came out of the shadows. One of them shouted at the unarmed blacks. Others pointed their muskets at the decks of the *Maquita*. It was clear that they were masters. The blacks were slaves.

2

The following winter, the coolest of seasons on St. Simon's Island, Chinwe lay on a mattress filled with straw, bundled in a threadbare blanket, waiting for the light of dawn. She shared the house with five other women, including Ifeoma.

Since the time of the mutiny, during all that had happened to her since, she had felt in herself a thread of steel, like the edge of a knife. She knew the thread would never break. She lay still, feeling the sadness of her life, but knowing that another day of work in the fields, the aching of her arms at night, would dull the sharpness of her pain. In the eye of her memory, she lived the mutiny again. She saw a vision of Cook as he stood in the doorway raising his knife, remembered the grounding of the ship and the strange black men who had stared at them in wonder and fear, and the whites, armed with muskets, who had brought up a cannon. A lieutenant of Okara had fired a musket from the deck of the *Maquita* and, when the white men fired back, three of the

Africans were killed. After that, the white men, together with the strange black men, fired the cannon, driving a hole through the hull of the ship, and as the ship's bilge filled, the Africans surrendered.

After the capture, Chinwe's spirit had been numb. Their captors had given the women and children clothes and guarded them carefully, day and night. The men and some of the boys had been taken off to prison, but Chinwe had kept Odili with her until they were bought by Massa Butler, a proud, cold man with a pallid skin and bright, pink cheeks.

A pistol shot had signaled the start of the auction at which the women and children were sold. They were stripped by a sweating, pig-eyed woman and Butler had walked among the rough, red men from backriver and swamp plantations, wearing finely tailored clothes, spotless breeches, pearly ruffles at his throat. He must have had some Ibo slaves because he spoke a little Ibo. He smiled at Odili, then faced Chinwe. "Were you and your people farmers?" he asked.

Chinwe said, "Yes."

Odili was silent.

Butler asked, "How would you like to work for me?"

"We want to go home," Chinwe said.

Butler nodded and passed along but at last he

125

bought Chinwe, Odili and Ifeoma.

Chinwe's thoughts turned to the island where they lived, in this land apart. It was less strange now than it had been at first and much of it was beautiful, the live oak forests, the flowers, lush beside the streams. In the evenings, she often saw tawny, white-tailed deer, standing still against the darkness of the pines. Chinwe had learned to love the moods of the water, the river, the Sound, sometimes placid as the Niger, sometimes flecked with angry waves.

She thought of the blacksmith shop by the river and the smith himself, a man remarkably like Azu. The smith was proud because he was valued, because he made many things and made them well, barrel hoops, fittings for harnesses and wagons, as well as shoes for the great dray horses. The smith loved Chinwe and Chinwe might someday love the smith, but marriage meant children and, unless her children could be free, she might never want to marry.

As the other women stirred, Chinwe knew that what she wanted most of all was hope. She had heard that some Americans of African descent, people who had once been slaves, were free. One-armed Jesse, one of Massa's favorites, had talked to Chinwe about these things, but instead of watching for a chance to escape, to push herself into the dark unknown, perhaps to fail, for a time

126

she would devote herself to learning what she could about this strange new land.

Chinwe dressed and stepped outside, took a path leading down to the shore. A heavy mist lay on Altamaha Sound. She heard the croak of a pelican, muffled by the fog, behind a stand of ghostly trees. The voices of children echoed in mist and, as Chinwe watched, the figures of the little ones began to emerge. One was Odili, running with another boy, as fast as he had run in their village, and Chinwe was certain, as she'd never been before, that one day she and Odili would be free.

The Author

Peter Burchard is the author of fifteen books. His stories and reviews have appeared in national magazines. In reviewing a recent book, *Whaleboat Raid, Publishers Weekly* rated him " . . . among the most able writers of our time." The New York *Times* has praised him highly, saying, ". . . he uses historical fact with skill" and describing him as having ". . . a splendid facility for characterization." He was a Guggenheim Fellow in 1966. In 1969, the *Library Journal* listed *Bimby* as one of the Best Books of the Year, calling it ". . . ballad-like in its simplicity."

First a writer, Burchard is also an artist and sailor. He has illustrated dozens of books, has crossed the Atlantic on merchant vessels, sailed in a number of ocean races and is the skipper of a small sloop named *Sarcelle*. His last book, *Ocean Race*, is a first-hand account of the 1976 Newport to Bermuda Race.